Likes & Lies

Michael Ferguson

Published by Michael Ferguson, 2024.

This is a work of fiction. Similarities to real people, places, or events are entirely coincidental.

LIKES & LIES

First edition. September 13, 2024.

ISBN: 979-8227830487

Written by Michael Ferguson.

Table of Contents

Chapter 1: The Perfect Image

The golden glow of the early morning sun filtered through the sheer curtains of Jess Turner's penthouse suite, casting long shadows across the polished marble floor. The view from her bedroom window was nothing short of spectacular—a sprawling cityscape dotted with skyscrapers, their glass facades catching the light like a million tiny mirrors. Jess leaned against the window frame, her gaze wandering over the horizon as she sipped from a steaming cup of artisanal coffee. It was a ritual she cherished, a moment of tranquility before the frenzy of her day began.

At eighteen, Jess was a social media sensation. With over ten million followers across various platforms, she had built an empire on the allure of perfection. Her feed was a curated masterpiece of opulent settings, glamorous events, and flawless selfies. Each post was meticulously crafted, a blend of high fashion, exotic locations, and an air of effortless sophistication. Jess knew how to sell the illusion of a perfect life, and her followers ate it up, envious of the world she presented.

Today, however, Jess wasn't focused on her usual routine of posting or engaging with her audience. She was preparing for a major collaboration with a luxury brand, a project that promised to solidify her status as an influencer and increase her already impressive earnings. Her manager, Lisa, had been pushing her hard to make sure everything was flawless. Jess's phone buzzed incessantly with reminders, and her calendar was packed with appointments and meetings. She had little time for anything beyond the endless grind of maintaining her online persona.

As she finished her coffee and set the mug on her sleek glass bedside table, Jess glanced at her reflection in the full-length mirror. Her skin was flawlessly smooth, her makeup expertly applied, and her outfit—a designer dress she had carefully chosen for the day's shoot—clung to her figure in all the right ways. It was a look she had perfected over countless hours of practice and self-discipline. She had learned early on that the key to success in her world was not just looking good but looking impeccably so.

Jess's phone buzzed again, pulling her out of her reverie. It was a text from Lisa, reminding her of an urgent briefing call. Jess sighed, her excitement for the day's events tempered by the pressure to meet the sky-high expectations set for her. She had become accustomed to the constant stream of messages, notifications, and demands that came with her fame. It was a double-edged sword—providing her with wealth and adoration while also encasing her in an unrelenting spotlight.

The call with Lisa was brief but intense. They discussed final details for the upcoming launch, the schedule for content releases, and the strategies for maximizing engagement. Jess listened carefully, her mind racing through the logistics and deadlines. Lisa's voice was a steady stream of instructions, and Jess nodded along, jotting down notes as she went. The pressure was palpable, but Jess had become adept at managing it, always with a smile and a sense of grace that belied the stress beneath.

After the call, Jess had a moment to herself before her next appointment. She decided to check her social media accounts, a habit she had developed out of both necessity and compulsion. Her feed was a testament to her success—likes, comments, and messages poured in from all corners of the globe. Her latest post, a glamorous snapshot from a recent event, had garnered thousands of interactions within hours. Jess felt a familiar rush of validation as she scrolled through the comments, each one an affirmation of her carefully crafted image.

But amidst the sea of adoring messages, one notification stood out. It was an anonymous message, the sender's name was simply "Unknown," and the content was startlingly direct: "I know what you did. Don't think your followers will save you." Jess's heart skipped a beat. She tapped the message, but the text was vague and unsettling, lacking any specific details or threats. Jess frowned, feeling a flicker of unease.

"Probably just another troll," she muttered to herself, trying to dismiss the growing sense of discomfort. She had dealt with her fair share of online negativity over the years, and the vast majority of it was meaningless. This message, however, felt different. It was personal and ominous in a way that made Jess's skin crawl.

Despite her attempts to brush it off, the message lingered in her thoughts throughout the morning. Jess threw herself into her work, focusing on her photo shoot and promotional content. She posed with practiced ease, smiling and laughing as the camera clicked away. The photographers and stylists complimented her, and Jess responded with the same warm, engaging demeanor that had won her so many fans. Yet, beneath the surface, her mind kept returning to the anonymous message.

As the day wore on, Jess's anxiety began to build. She couldn't shake the feeling that something was wrong, even though she had no concrete reason to be worried. She tried to distract herself by engaging with her followers and focusing on her work, but the unease remained. The message seemed to echo in her mind, a persistent reminder that not everything in her life was as perfect as it appeared.

By the evening, Jess was exhausted. She had managed to put on a brave face for her followers, but the weight of the anonymous threat hung over her like a dark cloud. She decided to call it a day and headed back to her penthouse. As she settled onto her plush couch, she took a deep breath and tried to relax. The city lights outside her window twinkled like a sea of stars, but they did little to ease the tension in her chest.

Her phone buzzed once more, interrupting her thoughts. It was a message from Lisa, reminding her about a live stream scheduled for the next day. Jess sighed and typed a quick response, acknowledging the reminder. As she set her phone aside, she glanced at her reflection in the large mirror across the room. The image of her perfect life seemed to mock her, a glossy facade concealing the growing cracks.

Jess knew she had to address the message, but she wasn't sure where to start. She considered discussing it with Lisa or perhaps her close friends, but she didn't want to alarm anyone unnecessarily. For now, she decided to keep it to herself, hoping it was just a misguided attempt at attention or a prank. She convinced herself that if she ignored it, it would go away.

As Jess prepared for bed, she couldn't shake the feeling of unease. She climbed under the soft, luxurious covers, trying to find comfort in the familiar surroundings of her penthouse. The city sounds drifted up from the streets below, a constant reminder of the bustling world outside. Jess's mind raced as she tried to push the anonymous message from her thoughts, but the lingering anxiety made it difficult to find rest.

Finally, she closed her eyes and tried to focus on the positive aspects of her life. She reminded herself of the accomplishments she had achieved, the millions of followers who admired her, and the opportunities that lay ahead. Jess knew that she had worked hard to get where she was, and she wasn't about to let a single unsettling message ruin her achievements.

As she drifted into a restless sleep, the message continued to haunt her dreams, a shadow lurking in the background of her otherwise glamorous life. Jess woke the next morning with a sense of apprehension that she couldn't quite shake. The day ahead was packed with responsibilities and expectations, but the anonymous threat remained a dark undercurrent that she couldn't ignore.

In the world of social media, where every moment was carefully curated and every post meticulously crafted, Jess Turner had built a perfect image. Yet, behind the façade of luxury and success, there were pressures and insecurities that she struggled to keep hidden. The anonymous message was a reminder that even in the spotlight, no one was truly safe from the shadows lurking just out of sight.

Jess prepared for her day with a practiced routine, trying to keep her mind focused on her work. As she moved through the various tasks and appointments, the message from the previous day lingered in the back of her mind, a subtle but persistent reminder that her perfect image was more fragile than she had ever imagined.

Jess Turner awoke the next morning to the sound of her phone vibrating incessantly on the nightstand. The digital buzz was persistent, dragging her from the deep slumber she had fought so hard to achieve. She groaned, reaching out with a tired hand to silence the intrusion. The early morning light, now a harsh reminder of reality, was already spilling into her room, chasing away the remnants of sleep.

After swiping the screen, Jess's eyes settled on a message notification. It was from a number she didn't recognize, and her heart skipped a beat as she remembered the anonymous threat from the day before. The message read: "Think you can ignore this? I'm just getting started. If you don't comply, your dirty little secrets will be all over the news."

Jess sat up abruptly, her mind racing. She had hoped that the previous day's message was nothing more than a prank, but the new message, more threatening and aggressive, confirmed that the situation was more serious than she had initially thought. The anxiety that had been brewing in the pit of her stomach now surged forward, making her pulse quicken.

She took a deep breath, trying to steady herself. The last thing she needed was to let this unknown threat disrupt her meticulously planned day. Jess had a busy schedule ahead of her, including a high-profile launch event and several media interviews. She had worked hard to get where she was, and she wasn't going to let an anonymous message derail her plans. Not today.

Determined not to let the message affect her, Jess got out of bed and began her morning routine. She went through the motions with practiced efficiency, applying her makeup with precision and selecting an outfit that would exude confidence and professionalism. Her appearance was part of her brand, and it was crucial that she maintained her flawless image, especially in the face of adversity.

As Jess stepped out of her penthouse and into the waiting car, she pushed the unsettling message to the back of her mind. The driver, an impeccably dressed man named Greg, greeted her with a polite nod. Jess offered a smile in return, though it didn't reach her eyes. Her mind was still preoccupied with the threat, but she knew she had to remain composed.

The car ride to the studio was a blur of cityscapes and fleeting thoughts. Jess tried to focus on the day's agenda, rehearsing her lines and responses for the interviews she had lined up. She mentally reviewed her social media posts, ensuring they were perfectly crafted to maintain her carefully curated image.

When Jess arrived at the studio, the bustling activity and cheerful chatter of the crew provided a welcome distraction. She was greeted by her team with smiles and enthusiastic hugs. Lisa, her manager, was already there, her presence a reassuring constant in Jess's whirlwind world.

"Morning, Jess!" Lisa exclaimed, handing her a stack of notes. "We have a lot to cover today. The launch event is going to be fantastic. I've got all the details laid out here."

Jess nodded, trying to focus on Lisa's words. She was grateful for Lisa's professionalism and support, especially on days like this when she felt anything but steady. As Lisa went over the schedule, Jess's phone buzzed again. She glanced at the screen and saw another anonymous message, but this time it was different: "You're running out of time. I suggest you start thinking about what you're willing to lose."

The message was unnervingly vague, yet it carried an ominous weight that Jess couldn't ignore. She fought the urge to panic, knowing that her reaction could potentially escalate the situation. Instead, she decided to keep her feelings in check and focus on the tasks at hand.

During the interviews and promotional events, Jess did her best to appear radiant and enthusiastic. Her charm and professionalism were evident, and the media seemed captivated by her presence. Despite her outward confidence, Jess couldn't fully shake the anxiety gnawing at her insides. Each buzz of her phone, each glance at her notifications, reminded her of the looming threat she had yet to confront.

After a long day of interviews and promotional activities, Jess finally had a moment to herself. She retreated to her dressing room, the sound of bustling activity outside a stark contrast to the quiet that enveloped her. The room was a sanctuary of calm, filled with plush furnishings and soft lighting. Jess sank into the comfortable chair, her mind still reeling from the day's events.

She took out her phone and read through the anonymous messages once more. They seemed to be deliberately designed to unsettle her, each one building on the fear and uncertainty of the last. Jess couldn't help but wonder who would want to target her in such a personal and invasive way. Was it someone from her past? An envious rival? Or perhaps someone she had wronged without realizing it?

With a sigh, Jess decided to take a proactive approach. She needed to find out who was behind these threats and put an end to it before it spiraled further. She couldn't afford to let this disrupt her life and career any longer. She composed a message to her closest friends and family, asking them to meet with her the following day. She intended to discuss the situation with them and seek their input, hoping that they might have some insight into the identity of the person targeting her.

As Jess sent out the messages, she couldn't shake the feeling that she was on the brink of something far more complicated than a simple prank. The anonymous threats seemed to be more than just idle threats—they felt personal, calculated, and deeply unsettling. She had always prided herself on her ability to handle the pressures of her public life, but this was different. The unknown nature of the threat made it all the more disturbing.

The night wore on, and Jess struggled to find rest. She tried to distract herself with television, but her mind kept wandering back to the messages and the growing sense of dread. The perfect image she had worked so hard to cultivate now seemed like a fragile veneer, concealing a world of anxiety and uncertainty beneath.

Eventually, exhaustion won out, and Jess fell into a restless sleep. Her dreams were filled with shadowy figures and cryptic messages, a reflection of the fear and uncertainty that had taken hold of her. When she awoke the next morning, she was determined to face the day with renewed resolve.

Jess spent the morning preparing for her meeting with her friends and family. She reviewed her notes and tried to calm her nerves. She knew that her loved ones might offer valuable perspectives or insights, and she hoped that by working together, they could uncover the identity of the person behind the threats.

As she drove to the meeting location, Jess's mind was a whirlwind of thoughts. The anxiety she felt was palpable, but she forced herself to focus on the task at hand. She couldn't let her fear control her actions; she needed to remain composed and proactive.

When Jess arrived at the café where she had arranged to meet her friends and family, she was greeted with warm smiles and concerned expressions. They had gathered around a large table, and Jess took a seat, feeling a mixture of relief and apprehension. She knew that sharing her fears with them was a risk, but she hoped it would lead to a solution.

The conversation began with casual pleasantries, but Jess soon steered it toward the reason for their meeting. She recounted the details of the anonymous messages and expressed her concerns about the threat. Her friends and family listened intently, their faces reflecting a range of emotions from shock to disbelief.

Rachel, Jess's best friend, was the first to speak. "Jess, this sounds really serious. Have you considered going to the police?"

Jess shook her head. "I'm not sure. I don't want to make a big deal out of it if it's just someone trying to scare me. But I also don't want to ignore it if it's something more serious."

Rachel nodded, her expression thoughtful. "I understand. But maybe it's worth looking into. There might be something we can do to help."

Jess's mother, Lisa, chimed in. "We should definitely take it seriously. This isn't something to brush off. Let's think about who might have a motive to target you."

As the discussion continued, Jess felt a sense of camaraderie and support from her loved ones. They brainstormed potential suspects and discussed various strategies for dealing with the threats. The meeting was productive, and Jess felt a glimmer of hope that they could find a resolution.

After the meeting, Jess returned to her penthouse with a renewed sense of determination. She knew that the road ahead would be challenging, but she was determined to confront the threats head-on. With the support of her friends and family, she felt more prepared to tackle the situation and uncover the truth behind the anonymous messages.

As Jess settled into her evening routine, she couldn't shake the feeling that she was on the cusp of a significant revelation. The threats were more than just a personal attack—they were a challenge to the carefully constructed world she had built. Jess was determined to face this challenge with courage and resilience, no matter where it led her.

The perfect image she had cultivated over the years now seemed more fragile than ever, but Jess was resolute. She would not let fear dictate her actions or allow the anonymous threats to control her life. With the support of her loved ones and a determination to uncover the truth, Jess was prepared to navigate the uncertainty and confront the unknown with strength and resolve.

Chapter 2: Unsettling Messages

Jess Turner sat at her marble-topped vanity, fingers hovering over her phone as the screen lit up with the latest notifications. The sunlight streamed through the large windows of her luxurious apartment, casting a warm glow over the elegant decor. It was a typical morning for the teen social media star, a blend of routine and the occasional surge of excitement as she checked her messages and posts.

Her following had grown substantially over the past few months, a testament to her relentless commitment to curating the perfect online persona. Jess had always been adept at portraying an ideal life, full of glamour, high-end fashion, and extravagant vacations. The likes and comments from her millions of followers were a daily affirmation of her success, a digital applause for her carefully crafted image.

But this morning, as Jess scrolled through her feed, something felt different. Her notifications were unusually quiet, and her latest posts hadn't received the usual flood of comments and likes. Frowning slightly, she tapped on the message icon, expecting to see the usual fan interactions and brand partnership inquiries. Instead, her eyes fell upon a new message from an anonymous account.

"I know your secrets, Jess. If you don't comply, I'll make sure everyone else does too. You've got 24 hours."

A chill ran down her spine as she read the message. The language was threatening, but Jess quickly brushed it off. She was used to the occasional troll or disgruntled follower making wild claims. This seemed like another attempt to get her attention or, worse, a desperate cry for relevance from someone trying to disrupt her perfect life.

With a dismissive swipe, Jess deleted the message and continued with her morning routine. She was in the middle of choosing an outfit for a photoshoot when her phone buzzed again. Another message from the same anonymous account.

"I've got proof. Don't think you can hide behind your filter forever. The clock is ticking."

Jess rolled her eyes and let out a frustrated sigh. The message was getting under her skin more than she cared to admit. She had always been diligent about keeping her personal life private, careful not to let anything slip that could tarnish her public image. Whoever was behind these messages was clearly trying to unsettle her, but she wasn't about to give them the satisfaction of knowing they'd succeeded.

Despite her best efforts to shake off the unease, the threat lingered in the back of her mind as she went through her day. She met with her manager, Linda, at their usual café for their weekly strategy session. Linda was a seasoned professional, adept at navigating the turbulent waters of social media fame. She had been with Jess since the beginning, and her calm demeanor was one of the few constants in Jess's otherwise unpredictable life.

"Hey, Linda," Jess greeted as she took a seat at their reserved table. "You won't believe what happened this morning."

Linda glanced up from her coffee, her expression a mix of curiosity and concern. "What's going on?"

Jess recounted the anonymous messages, trying to keep her tone casual. "Some random account sent me these creepy messages threatening to reveal secrets if I don't do something. I don't know what their deal is, but it seems like just another troll trying to get a rise out of me."

Linda's eyebrows knitted together as she listened. "Have you thought about reporting it to the platform?"

"I did, but it doesn't seem like there's much they can do," Jess replied, shrugging. "Besides, I don't want to make a big deal out of it and give them more attention."

Linda nodded thoughtfully. "I understand. But it's important to be cautious. These things can sometimes escalate, and it's better to be prepared. We should keep an eye on it and see if anything else comes up."

Jess agreed, though she couldn't shake the nagging feeling that this was more than just a harmless prank. As the day wore on, she found herself increasingly distracted by the looming threat. She tried to focus on her work, attending meetings, and preparing for her upcoming promotional events, but the constant hum of anxiety made it difficult to concentrate.

That evening, Jess decided to take a break and unwind with her best friend, Rachel. They had planned a casual dinner at a trendy new restaurant, a chance to catch up and enjoy some downtime away from the pressures of social media. Jess hoped that the evening would help her clear her mind and regain some sense of normalcy.

Rachel arrived at the restaurant, her bright smile and infectious energy a welcome distraction from Jess's worries.

They exchanged hugs and took their seats at a cozy table by the window. The warm ambiance and delicious aroma of the restaurant provided a temporary respite from Jess's anxiety.

"So, how's everything going?" Rachel asked, her eyes twinkling with genuine interest. "You seem a little off today."

Jess hesitated for a moment before deciding to confide in her friend. "I got these weird messages this morning. Someone's threatening to reveal secrets if I don't comply with whatever they want. It's probably nothing, but it's been bugging me all day."

Rachel's expression shifted from curiosity to concern. "That sounds really unsettling. Have you talked to anyone about it?"

"Just Linda," Jess replied. "She thinks it might be a troll, but it's still bothering me. I don't want to make a big fuss if it's nothing, but I also don't want to ignore it if it turns out to be serious."

Rachel nodded sympathetically. "I get it. If you need anything or want to talk about it more, I'm here for you."

Jess appreciated Rachel's support, though a part of her remained wary. The anonymous messages had cast a shadow over what was supposed to be a relaxing evening. As they chatted and enjoyed their meal, Jess couldn't shake the feeling that something was lurking just beneath the surface, waiting to disrupt her seemingly perfect life.

By the time they finished their dinner and said their goodbyes, Jess was mentally exhausted. She returned to her apartment, her mind still preoccupied with the cryptic messages. She knew she had to take some action, but the threat of a possible scandal loomed large, and she wasn't sure how to handle it.

As Jess prepared for bed, she took one last look at her phone, half-expecting to see another message from the anonymous account. To her relief, there were no new notifications. She set her phone on her nightstand, determined to push the unsettling thoughts aside and get some rest.

But as she lay in bed, her mind continued to race. The threats from the anonymous account felt like a dark cloud hanging over her, and despite her best efforts to ignore them, she couldn't shake the feeling that something was coming. The pressure of maintaining her flawless image had always been a burden, but now it seemed to be morphing into something far more sinister.

Jess closed her eyes and took a deep breath, trying to calm her racing thoughts. Tomorrow would bring new challenges, and she needed to be ready to face whatever came her way. Little did she know that the unsettling messages were just the beginning of a far more complex and dangerous situation.

As she drifted off to sleep, Jess couldn't help but wonder what lay ahead. The digital world she had carefully constructed was starting to crack, and she was about to find herself at the center of a storm that threatened to unravel everything she had worked so hard to build.

The following morning, Jess Turner awoke to the buzz of her phone, signaling the start of a new day filled with the usual demands of her social media career. But the looming presence of the anonymous threats still hung heavy on her mind. The once-glamorous facade of her life now felt tainted by a sense of dread. She had a busy day ahead, with several brand meetings and content creation sessions scheduled, but the mysterious messages had shifted her focus.

As Jess made her way through her morning routine, her mind remained preoccupied with the cryptic threats. She had been advised by Linda, her manager, to keep a low profile and avoid drawing any further attention to the situation. But Jess couldn't ignore the gnawing feeling that something more sinister was at play. If the anonymous account was intent on causing trouble, she needed to understand the scope of their claims and figure out a way to protect her reputation.

The first order of business was a meeting with her team at their downtown office. Jess arrived to find Linda already at her desk, going over a stack of documents. Her assistant, Emma, greeted her with a warm smile, though Jess could tell her assistant was keenly aware of the tension in the air.

"Morning, Jess," Linda said, looking up from her work. "How are you holding up?"

"I'm managing," Jess replied, taking a seat. "But I'm concerned about these messages. I want to address them head-on before they get out of hand."

Linda's expression grew serious. "I understand, but our priority should be to manage the situation without escalating it. The last thing we want is for this to become a public spectacle."

Jess nodded, though she wasn't entirely convinced. "I get that. But we need to know what we're dealing with. If there's any truth to these threats, I want to get ahead of it."

Linda leaned back in her chair, considering Jess's words. "Alright, here's what we'll do. We'll monitor the situation closely, make sure the platform is aware of the threats, and keep a low profile for now. Meanwhile, I'd recommend focusing on your scheduled content and engagements. Distracting yourself with work might help keep your mind off the situation."

Jess agreed to the plan, though her resolve to investigate remained strong. After the meeting, she took a moment to collect her thoughts before diving into her busy day. Her first appointment was a brand collaboration meeting with a high-profile cosmetics company. She put on her best smile, navigating through the scripted pitch and posing for photos as if everything were normal. But beneath the surface, her thoughts kept drifting back to the anonymous threats and their implications.

The meeting went smoothly, and Jess was able to put on a facade of composure. But once it was over, she retreated to her private office, seeking solace in the quiet space. She knew she had to act quickly and gather information about the disturbing messages. Her initial reaction was to reach out to her closest friends and family, starting with those who were most likely to be involved or have insight into the situation.

Jess picked up her phone and dialed Rachel's number. She needed to know if her friend had any information or if she was aware of anything unusual. Rachel answered on the first ring, her voice cheerful but laced with a hint of curiosity.

"Hey Jess! How's it going?"

"Hey Rachel," Jess replied, trying to keep her tone casual. "I wanted to touch base about something. You know, those weird messages I told you about? I've been getting more of them, and they're starting to get really specific."

Rachel's tone shifted to concern. "Oh no, that's not good. What are they saying?"

"They're insinuating that I'm involved in some local crimes. It's pretty serious," Jess explained. "I'm trying to figure out if there's any truth to it or if it's just someone trying to cause trouble."

Rachel hesitated before responding. "I haven't heard anything like that, but I can ask around and see if anyone else has. Maybe it's someone trying to get attention."

"I appreciate it," Jess said. "Let me know if you hear anything. And if you come across anything that seems suspicious, don't hesitate to tell me."

They wrapped up the call, and Jess couldn't shake the feeling that Rachel's response had been somewhat guarded. She pushed the thought aside, deciding to reach out to her family next. They had always been supportive, and Jess hoped they might have some insights into the situation.

She called her mother, Karen, who answered with her usual warmth. "Hi, Jess! How's everything going?"

"Hi Mom," Jess said, her voice betraying a hint of anxiety. "I need to talk to you about something. I've been getting some strange messages online. They're accusing me of being involved in some local crimes."

Karen's voice took on a tone of alarm. "Oh, Jess, that sounds serious. Are you okay? What kind of crimes are they talking about?"

"I'm not sure yet," Jess admitted. "The messages are really vague, but they're making it seem like I'm connected to something criminal. I'm trying to figure out if there's any truth to it or if it's just a prank."

Karen sighed heavily. "I haven't heard anything about you being involved in anything like that. I'll keep my ears open and let you know if I come across anything. Just be careful, okay?"

"I will, Mom," Jess said, feeling a bit reassured. "Thanks for your support. I'll keep you updated."

As Jess ended the call, she couldn't shake the feeling that something was off. The messages were clearly intended to disrupt her life, but why? Who could want to target her so specifically? The questions lingered in her mind as she moved on to her next task, trying to focus on her work.

The day passed in a blur of meetings and content creation, but Jess's thoughts remained preoccupied with the anonymous threats. As evening approached, she felt a growing sense of urgency to get to the bottom of the situation. She needed to be proactive and gather as much information as possible.

She decided to visit her brother, Alex, who lived nearby. Alex was a tech-savvy individual and might be able to provide some insights into the digital aspect of the threats. Jess hoped that he could help her trace the origin of the anonymous messages or at least offer some technical advice.

When Jess arrived at Alex's apartment, she was greeted with a warm hug and a welcoming smile. Alex led her into the living room, where they settled onto the couch. Jess quickly explained the situation, showing him the threatening messages she had received.

Alex studied the messages carefully, his brow furrowing in concentration. "These are pretty sophisticated," he said, scrolling through the texts. "Whoever is behind this knows how to cover their tracks. The account is completely anonymous, and there's no direct link to any identifiable information."

Jess sighed in frustration. "That's what I feared. I need to know if there's any way to trace these messages or figure out who might be behind them."

Alex nodded thoughtfully. "I can try to run some analysis on the account and see if we can get any leads. It might not be easy, but we'll give it a shot."

Jess felt a glimmer of hope as Alex began his investigation. She spent the next few hours at his apartment, discussing possible leads and reviewing any information that could help identify the anonymous sender. Despite their best efforts, the account remained frustratingly elusive.

As the night wore on, Jess began to feel the weight of the day's events catching up with her. The stress of the threats, combined with the constant pressure to maintain her public image, had taken a toll. She thanked Alex for his help and headed home, feeling both physically and emotionally drained.

Back at her apartment, Jess tried to relax and clear her mind. She knew that tomorrow would bring new challenges and that she needed to be prepared. The anonymous messages had already disrupted her life, but she refused to let them control her. She was determined to get to the bottom of the situation and reclaim her sense of normalcy.

As she lay in bed, Jess replayed the events of the day in her mind. The unsettling messages, the responses from her friends and family, and the technical analysis with Alex all painted a picture of a situation that was growing increasingly complex. The more she learned, the more she realized that she was dealing with something far beyond a simple prank.

Jess closed her eyes and took a deep breath, trying to calm her racing thoughts. She knew that she needed to stay focused and take control of the situation. The threats had exposed vulnerabilities in her carefully curated world, and she was determined to address them head-on.

Little did she know, the storm that had begun with a few cryptic messages was only the beginning. As Jess prepared for the challenges ahead, she was about to uncover a web of deceit that would test her resolve and force her to confront the darkest corners of her life and career. The journey to unravel the truth would not only challenge her sense of self but also redefine her understanding of trust and deception.

Chapter 3: The Trail of Lies

The glow of the morning sun streamed through the curtains of Jess Turner's bedroom, casting a warm hue over the meticulously curated space. Despite the idyllic surroundings, Jess felt a gnawing unease deep within her. The previous days had been a whirlwind of anxiety, uncertainty, and sleepless nights, all stemming from the anonymous threats that had begun to plague her social media accounts. What was once a sanctuary of carefully crafted images and polished posts had transformed into a battleground of deceit.

Jess had spent the night going through the disturbing messages once again, trying to find any clue that could link them to someone she knew. The more she examined them, the more she realized that the threats were not just random; they were calculated and deliberate. Each message seemed to reveal a deeper layer of her personal life, hinting at secrets that only someone close to her could know.

As she prepared for the day ahead, Jess's thoughts were consumed by one question: Who could be behind this? The messages were too specific to be from a random troll. She had a feeling that the anonymous account was tied to her past, and she was determined to uncover the truth.

After a quick breakfast, Jess set out to meet her private investigator, Mark, whom she had hired to help trace the origins of the anonymous messages. Mark was a no-nonsense professional with a reputation for getting results, and Jess hoped his expertise would shed some light on the situation.

They met at a small café near Mark's office. Jess arrived early, her nerves on edge as she waited for him to show up. The café was quiet, its ambient noise providing a stark contrast to the turmoil that was brewing in Jess's mind. When Mark walked in, he gave her a reassuring nod, his demeanor calm and collected.

"Jess, good to see you," Mark said, taking a seat across from her. "Let's get right to it. What have you got for me?"

Jess handed over her phone, showing him the various messages and posts that had been causing her distress. Mark studied the screen with a practiced eye, his expression growing more serious as he reviewed the content.

"These messages are quite detailed," he remarked, scrolling through the texts. "It's clear that whoever is behind this has done their homework. They're leveraging personal information to make these threats more believable."

"I know," Jess said, her voice tinged with frustration. "I need to find out who's behind this. It feels like it's someone from my past, but I can't pinpoint who."

Mark nodded thoughtfully. "We'll start by analyzing the digital footprint of the anonymous account. I'll also look into any potential connections between these messages and your known associates. It's possible that someone from your past might be involved."

Jess felt a flicker of hope as Mark began to work. She watched him as he made notes and asked questions, his focus unwavering. It was a small comfort to know that she had someone dedicated to unraveling the mystery.

While Mark worked, Jess couldn't help but think about her social circle and the people closest to her. There were a few individuals who had access to her personal life and could potentially have a motive for targeting her. Her mind wandered to Rachel, her longtime best friend, who had seemed somewhat evasive when Jess spoke to her recently. Although Rachel had claimed innocence, Jess couldn't shake the feeling that she might know more than she was letting on.

In addition to Rachel, Jess thought about her family. They had always been a pillar of support for her, but recent events had revealed cracks in their support. Her father's erratic behavior and her mother's cryptic responses had raised questions about their involvement. The thought of them being involved in any way was distressing, but Jess knew she had to consider all possibilities.

After an hour of intense analysis, Mark looked up from his laptop with a thoughtful expression. "I've managed to trace some of the digital activity linked to the anonymous account. There's a pattern to the IP addresses and the way the messages are structured. It looks like the account was created using a series of proxy servers to mask the true location."

Jess's heart sank. "So it's not going to be easy to track down the person responsible?"

Mark shook his head. "Not necessarily. The proxies can help us narrow down the general location, and if we're lucky, we might find additional clues in the account's activity. But it's going to take some time and effort."

Jess nodded, trying to maintain her composure. "What's our next step?"

"We'll continue to dig into the account's activity and see if we can uncover any connections," Mark said. "In the meantime, it might be worth revisiting your social circle. Sometimes the answers lie closer to home than we expect."

Jess took Mark's advice to heart. As she left the café, she felt a renewed sense of determination. She needed to be proactive and gather as much information as possible. The threats had shaken her world, but she was determined to regain control and uncover the truth.

Back at her apartment, Jess decided to revisit her interactions with her closest friends and family. She started with Rachel, arranging a meet-up to discuss the situation further. Although Rachel had seemed concerned during their last conversation, Jess felt a pressing need to delve deeper.

They met at a local park, a place that had once been their favorite hangout spot. The serene environment was a stark contrast to the tension that lingered between them. Jess and Rachel sat on a park bench, surrounded by the soothing sounds of nature.

"Rachel, I need to be honest with you," Jess began, her voice steady. "I've been feeling really uneasy about everything that's been happening. I know you said you'd look into things, but I can't shake the feeling that something's off."

Rachel looked down, her fingers fidgeting with the strap of her purse. "Jess, I understand. This whole situation is just so messed up. I really don't know what to tell you."

Jess studied Rachel's face, searching for any signs of deception. "You seem a bit on edge. Is there something you're not telling me?"

Rachel hesitated, her eyes darting around the park. "I swear, I don't know anything more. But... I've been hearing rumors about someone who might have a grudge against you. It's just whispers, though. I don't know who it could be."

Jess felt a surge of frustration. "I need more than just whispers, Rachel. I need to know if there's any truth to these rumors. If you hear anything concrete, you have to let me know."

Rachel nodded, her expression earnest. "I promise I will. I just want this to be over as much as you do."

As Jess left the park, she couldn't shake the feeling that Rachel's response had been less than reassuring. It was possible that Rachel was genuinely unaware of the full extent of the situation, but Jess couldn't ignore the nagging suspicion that there was more to uncover.

With a heavy heart, Jess turned her attention to her family. She decided to have a candid conversation with her mother, Karen, about the recent developments. Although Jess had already spoken to Karen, she felt the need to revisit the discussion and probe deeper.

They met at a cozy café that Karen frequented. Jess was relieved to see her mother's familiar face, though she couldn't ignore the tension that had developed between them. Karen greeted her with a warm hug, but Jess could sense an undercurrent of unease.

"Mom, thanks for meeting me," Jess said as they settled at a table. "I need to talk to you about something important."

Karen's expression grew serious. "Of course, Jess. What's on your mind?"

"I've been getting more of those threatening messages, and I'm starting to think that they're connected to someone from my past," Jess said, her voice tinged with worry. "I've been trying to piece together any potential leads, but I need your help."

Karen looked thoughtful, her eyes searching Jess's face. "I wish I could offer more help. I've been thinking about it, and I don't know if there's anything I can add that would be useful."

Jess's frustration bubbled to the surface. "Mom, I need to know if there's anything you might have heard or seen that could be relevant. Even the smallest detail could make a difference."

Karen sighed heavily. "Alright, Jess. There's something I didn't mention before. A while back, there were some issues with Amanda, a girl you used to be friends with. She had been spreading rumors and causing trouble. I didn't think it was related, but now I'm wondering."

Jess's heart raced at the mention of Amanda. "Amanda? Why didn't you tell me about this before?"

"I didn't want to alarm you," Karen explained. "I thought it was just teenage drama, but now it seems like it might be more serious."

Jess felt a mix of relief and frustration. The connection to Amanda seemed like a significant lead, but the delay in her mother's disclosure added another layer of complexity to the situation. Jess resolved to dig deeper into Amanda's involvement and see if there was a link between her and the anonymous threats.

As Jess left the café, she felt a renewed sense of determination. The pieces of the puzzle were slowly starting to come together, but there was still much work to be done. She needed to connect the dots between Amanda and the anonymous account, and she was determined to uncover the truth, no matter how deep the trail of lies might go.

Jess Turner stared at the cluttered desk in her bedroom, the room dimly lit by the desk lamp casting eerie shadows on the walls. Her laptop's screen glowed with a list of the unsettling messages and cryptic posts she had been receiving. The list seemed endless, each line a painful reminder of the online torment she was enduring. Jess's fingers hovered over the keyboard as she attempted to piece together the puzzle, her mind racing through the inconsistencies she had uncovered.

Her investigation had taken a turn she hadn't anticipated. The more she dug into the origins of the threatening messages, the more she found herself entangled in a web of deceit and hidden motives. The anonymous account that had been taunting her with threats had links to her past—someone who knew her well enough to strike at her vulnerabilities. But who?

In the hours leading up to this point, Jess had discovered that the messages were not random but had a systematic pattern. Each message seemed to reveal a new detail about her life, one that could only come from someone close to her. Her initial suspicions about her social circle were starting to solidify, and she couldn't shake the feeling that there were people around her who were not being entirely honest.

The first step of her investigation had led her to scrutinize her family's recent behavior. Jess's family had always been her support system, the ones who stood by her through the highs and lows of her social media fame. But recently, she had noticed subtle changes—her mother's evasiveness, her father's uncharacteristic irritability. Her brother, Leo, had become distant, preferring to spend time away from home.

Her thoughts were interrupted by a soft knock on her door. Jess looked up to see her mother, Emily, standing in the doorway, her expression a mixture of concern and curiosity.

"Jess, honey, are you okay?" Emily's voice was gentle but laced with an undercurrent of tension.

Jess took a deep breath, trying to mask the anxiety she felt. "I'm fine, Mom. Just working on something."

Emily's gaze lingered on the mess of papers and the open laptop. "You've been up here a lot lately. Maybe you should take a break."

Jess forced a smile, her heart racing. "I can't afford to take a break right now. I need to get to the bottom of these messages."

Emily nodded, though Jess could see the concern in her eyes. "Well, if you need anything, I'm here."

As Emily left, Jess felt a pang of guilt. Her mother's concern was genuine, but Jess couldn't shake the feeling that there was more beneath the surface. Her mother's reaction had been oddly subdued, and Jess couldn't help but wonder if there was something she wasn't being told.

Turning back to her laptop, Jess revisited the message logs. The anonymous account had a history of sporadic activity, only becoming active recently with the threats. Jess had managed to trace some of the IP addresses associated with the account, leading her to suspect that the person behind it had some local connections.

The messages had included details about her family, and Jess was particularly disturbed by one that mentioned her brother, Leo. It was a subtle but chilling comment about how her brother was caught in the crossfire of the drama. Jess had brushed it off initially, but now, in light of her brother's recent behavior, she couldn't ignore the possibility that he might be involved or, at the very least, a part of the larger scheme.

She decided to confront Leo. Jess knew it was a delicate matter—accusing someone close to her without concrete evidence could jeopardize their relationship, but she couldn't ignore her growing suspicions.

Leo was in his room, engrossed in his video game, the soft hum of the console filling the air. Jess knocked on his door before entering. He barely glanced up from his screen.

"Hey, Jess. What's up?"

"Got a minute?" Jess asked, trying to keep her voice calm.

Leo paused the game and looked at her with a puzzled expression. "Sure. What's going on?"

Jess took a seat on the edge of his bed, her mind racing as she tried to frame her questions carefully. "I've been getting some weird messages online, and they're starting to mention family stuff. I was wondering if you've noticed anything strange lately."

Leo's brow furrowed. "Like what kind of stuff?"

Jess hesitated, then decided to be upfront. "They've been mentioning you—saying things that seem off. I just wanted to make sure everything's okay with you."

Leo shifted uncomfortably. "I haven't seen anything weird. Maybe it's just a prank or something."

Jess studied his face, searching for any sign of dishonesty. "Are you sure? I mean, you know I wouldn't bring this up if it wasn't serious."

Leo met her gaze, his expression earnest. "I promise, Jess. I haven't done anything, and I haven't seen anything that would be connected to those messages."

Jess nodded, though she wasn't entirely convinced. Leo seemed sincere, but she knew better than to take things at face value. There was still something unsettling about his response, something that didn't sit right with her.

As she left Leo's room, Jess's thoughts were tumultuous. Her family had always been her rock, but now she was questioning their honesty and involvement in the situation. She needed to dig deeper, and that meant looking beyond just her family.

Her next focus was her best friend, Rachel. Rachel had been Jess's confidant through thick and thin, but the recent changes in her behavior had raised red flags. Jess decided to visit Rachel, hoping to get a clearer understanding of where she stood.

Rachel's apartment was a cozy space, filled with mementos of their shared memories. Jess had always felt at ease here, but tonight, the atmosphere felt different—charged with an unspoken tension. Rachel greeted her with a warm hug, but Jess could sense a layer of unease beneath the surface.

"Hey, Jess! What's up?" Rachel's voice was slightly higher than usual, her smile not quite reaching her eyes.

"I just wanted to talk," Jess said, taking a seat on the couch. "I've been dealing with these threats online, and I've noticed some things that don't add up. I need to know if you've seen or heard anything that might help."

Rachel's face paled slightly. "I haven't really been paying attention to social media lately. I've been swamped with school and stuff."

Jess studied Rachel's face, noticing her shifting gaze and fidgeting hands. "Rachel, you know I value our friendship. If there's anything you're hiding or if you know something, I need you to be honest with me."

Rachel bit her lip, looking conflicted. "Jess, I—I don't know what to say. I've been getting some weird messages too, but I didn't think much of it. I thought maybe it was just a coincidence."

Jess leaned forward, her voice low and serious. "Rachel, if there's anything you're not telling me, now's the time to come clean. This isn't just about me anymore. It's about everyone who might be involved."

Rachel's eyes welled up with tears. "I'm sorry, Jess. I didn't want to worry you. I've been getting these messages too, and they're not just about you. They mention things about our friends and family, but I didn't think they were related."

Jess's heart sank. The confirmation that Rachel was also receiving strange messages only complicated things further. "Why didn't you tell me sooner?"

Rachel wiped her eyes, her voice trembling. "I was scared. I thought if I ignored it, it would go away. But now, seeing how serious this is, I realize I should have said something."

Jess took a deep breath, trying to process the new information. "We need to figure out what's going on and who's behind all this. I'm starting to think that there's someone from our past who's pulling the strings."

Rachel nodded, her expression a mixture of fear and determination. "I'll help you in any way I can. I don't want to be caught up in this mess either."

The two friends spent the next few hours poring over the messages and trying to piece together any connections. Jess couldn't shake the feeling that the threads of deceit were tightening around her, and with every revelation, the stakes grew higher.

As Jess left Rachel's apartment, she felt a mix of frustration and resolve. The investigation was far from over, and the discrepancies in her family's and friends' behavior only fueled her determination to uncover the truth. She knew that the trail of lies led deeper than she had initially imagined, and she was prepared to confront whatever came next.

The night was quiet as Jess made her way back home, her mind racing with thoughts of betrayal and deceit. The path ahead was uncertain, but Jess was resolute in her quest for the truth. She couldn't afford to let the lies win.

Chapter 4: Crumbling Facades

The sun had barely begun to rise when Jess Turner woke up that morning, her mind already preoccupied with the turmoil that had become her life. The soft, golden light filtering through the curtains did little to brighten the dark cloud hanging over her. Her recent investigations had only revealed more questions and deeper mistrust among those she had always relied on. The world she had once thought was stable and trustworthy was now unraveling before her eyes.

After a restless night filled with half-formed dreams of betrayal and deception, Jess stumbled out of bed and dragged herself to the bathroom. Her reflection in the mirror showed a tired face, with dark circles under her eyes that had become all too familiar. She splashed cold water on her face, hoping it would wake her from this nightmare, but it only seemed to solidify the reality she was facing.

Her phone buzzed on the counter, a reminder of the ever-present world of social media she had tried to escape from. Jess picked it up with a sigh and saw a new message from Rachel. It was a simple text: "Can we talk? I think we need to clear the air." Jess frowned. Rachel's previous evasiveness and nervousness had left Jess feeling unsettled, and this message did little to reassure her.

Despite her reservations, Jess knew she needed to confront Rachel to get to the bottom of things. She quickly dressed in a pair of jeans and a hoodie, not in the mood for her usual polished appearance. A quick breakfast and a hurried exit later, she was on her way to Rachel's apartment, her heart pounding with a mix of anxiety and determination.

Rachel lived in a modest, two-bedroom apartment a few blocks away from Jess's place. The building was old but well-kept, with a welcoming atmosphere that had always made Jess feel at ease. Today, however, the familiarity of the place felt different, tinged with an uncomfortable edge. Jess took the elevator to Rachel's floor and knocked on her door.

Rachel opened it with a tired smile that didn't quite reach her eyes. "Hey, Jess. Thanks for coming over."

Jess followed Rachel inside, noticing how Rachel's apartment seemed unusually cluttered, with papers and books strewn about. It was clear that Rachel had been preoccupied with something—maybe the same things that had been troubling Jess.

"Thanks for inviting me," Jess said as she took a seat on the couch. "I wanted to talk about what's been going on. I feel like there's more to this than we've been able to figure out."

Rachel nodded, sitting down beside Jess. "Yeah, I've been thinking about it a lot too. There's definitely something weird going on, and I'm sorry if I've made you feel like I wasn't being honest."

Jess leaned forward, her gaze fixed on Rachel. "I need you to be completely honest with me. These messages—there's something not right about them. I feel like we're missing a piece of the puzzle. What else have you been keeping from me?"

Rachel's expression grew more serious. "I wasn't sure how to tell you this, but I've been getting more than just the occasional weird message. Some of them have been really threatening, and they seem to be coming from people who know a lot about our lives."

Jess's heart raced. "What kind of threats are we talking about?"

Rachel hesitated, then pulled out her phone and opened a message thread. She handed it to Jess, who skimmed through the chilling messages. They were not just cryptic but direct, mentioning personal details and hinting at dangerous consequences if Rachel didn't cooperate.

Jess's stomach churned. "These are intense. Why didn't you tell me sooner?"

Rachel looked pained. "I didn't want to add to your stress, and honestly, I was scared. I thought it was just a prank or something at first, but then the messages got worse. I didn't know who to turn to, and I didn't want to drag you into it."

Jess shook her head, frustration and concern mingling in her voice. "Rachel, we're in this together. If someone is targeting both of us, we need to figure out who it is and why. We can't let this scare us into silence."

Rachel nodded, tears forming in her eyes. "I know. I should have told you earlier. I've been so on edge lately that I didn't think straight. I've been trying to piece things together too, but it feels like I'm hitting dead ends."

Jess took a deep breath, trying to calm her racing thoughts. "We need to look at everyone in our circle, see if there's anyone who might have a reason to target us. This isn't just about us anymore; it's affecting everyone around us."

Rachel wiped her eyes and nodded. "Okay, let's do it. Where do we start?"

Jess thought for a moment. "We need to consider everyone who might have a grudge against us or who might benefit from seeing us fall. That includes our friends, acquaintances, and even people from our past. Anyone who might have a motive."

Rachel's face grew pale. "What about Amanda?"

Jess looked at Rachel, her eyes narrowing. "Amanda? You mean the influencer from back in the day?"

Rachel nodded. "Yeah, she's someone I've been thinking about. I know you two had a falling out, and she might still be holding a grudge."

Jess's mind raced. Amanda had been a close friend before their relationship soured over a series of misunderstandings and competitive tensions. The fallout had been public and messy, and Amanda had since become a rival in the influencer world. Could she be behind the threats?

"Maybe," Jess said slowly. "But we need more than just suspicion. We need concrete evidence."

Rachel sighed. "I'll dig through my messages and see if there's any pattern or connection to Amanda. In the meantime, we should also look into anyone else who might have a reason to harm us."

Jess agreed, and they spent the next few hours going through their old contacts and social media connections. They analyzed past interactions, old arguments, and anyone who might have had a motive to target them. Each piece of information was scrutinized and cross-referenced with the threats they had received.

As they worked, Jess's thoughts kept drifting back to her family. The recent changes in their behavior had been unsettling, and the secrets she had uncovered about them only added to her growing unease. She knew she had to address these issues head-on, but she was unsure how to approach the situation without causing further rifts.

Her father's behavior, in particular, had been increasingly erratic. His recent outbursts and irrational decisions had raised concerns. Jess couldn't ignore the possibility that his behavior might be linked to the ongoing crisis, especially with the financial troubles he had hinted at.

Later that afternoon, Jess returned home and found her father in the living room, engrossed in paperwork. He looked up as she entered, his expression a mix of weariness and distraction.

"Hey, Dad," Jess said, trying to sound casual. "Do you have a minute to talk?"

Her father glanced at her and nodded. "Sure, Jess. What's on your mind?"

Jess took a deep breath, steeling herself. "I've been thinking about everything that's been happening lately, and I feel like there's something I'm not seeing. I need to understand what's going on, especially with your recent behavior."

Her father's face hardened slightly. "What do you mean by that?"

Jess hesitated. "I've noticed you've been more stressed and distracted lately. And there's been talk about financial issues. Is there something you're not telling me?"

Her father's expression softened, and he sighed heavily. "Jess, it's complicated. There have been some financial problems, but it's not something I wanted to burden you with. I've been trying to handle it on my own."

Jess's heart sank. "Dad, if there's something going on, I need to know. We're all in this together, and keeping secrets isn't helping anyone."

Her father looked at her, his eyes filled with a mix of regret and frustration. "I didn't want to worry you. I thought I could fix things before you noticed. But since you're asking, yes, there have been issues. Some investments went bad, and we're struggling to keep up with the bills."

Jess felt a pang of guilt. She had been so focused on her own problems that she hadn't fully considered the impact on her family. "Why didn't you tell me sooner?"

Her father shook his head. "I didn't want to add to your stress. You have enough to deal with right now. I should have been more open about it, but I was afraid of how you'd react."

Jess tried to process the information. "Do you think this could be connected to the threats I've been receiving? Is there someone who might be using our financial issues against us?"

Her father's face grew pale. "It's possible. There's been some strange behavior from a few people lately. I didn't want to believe it, but now that you mention it, there might be a connection."

Jess nodded, her mind racing with the implications. The financial strain on her family could be a motive for someone to target them. She knew she had to dig deeper and uncover any links between their financial problems and the ongoing threats.

As she left her father's study, Jess felt a renewed sense of determination. The facade of her seemingly perfect life was crumbling, but she was committed to uncovering the truth.

The pieces of the puzzle were falling into place, and Jess was determined to piece them together, no matter how painful the truth might be.

The following days were a blur of frantic activity as Jess continued her investigation. She balanced her time between scrutinizing Rachel's findings, delving into her family's financial troubles, and trying to maintain some semblance of normalcy in her public life. The pressure was relentless, but Jess was determined to find answers.

Her relationship with Rachel remained strained but cooperative. Rachel continued to dig through her contacts, looking for any link to Amanda or other potential suspects. Jess focused on her family, trying to piece together the financial issues and their possible connection to the threats.

The investigation was taking a toll on Jess's mental and emotional well-being. The constant uncertainty and the weight of the secrets she was uncovering left her feeling isolated and overwhelmed. Yet, through it all, she remained resolute in her quest for the truth.

As Jess prepared for another day of searching for answers, she couldn't shake the feeling that she was on the verge of discovering something significant. The crumbling facades of her seemingly perfect life were revealing hidden truths, and Jess was determined to confront them head-on.

In the midst of the chaos, Jess found solace in small moments of clarity and resolve. She knew that the path to the truth would be fraught with challenges, but she was ready to face them, no matter how difficult or painful they might be. The fight for her reputation, her trust, and her sense of self had only just begun.

Jess Turner sat alone in her room, the walls closing in with every passing minute. The sun had set, leaving her with only the soft glow of her desk lamp to illuminate her thoughts. Her mind was racing, filled with fragments of conversations, troubling messages, and the unsettling feeling that everything she once believed to be true was now under scrutiny. The secrets she was uncovering were like cracks in a once-solid foundation, and Jess feared the entire structure might come crashing down.

She had just finished her meeting with Rachel, where she had hoped to gain clarity, but instead, she left with more questions than answers. Rachel's nervous demeanor and her cryptic admissions had only added to Jess's anxiety. If Rachel was hiding something, it only fueled Jess's suspicion that there was more to this situation than met the eye.

As Jess pondered her next steps, her phone buzzed with a notification. It was another message, this one from an unknown number. The text was short but chilling: "You're getting closer, Jess. Keep digging and you'll find the truth, but be careful what you wish for."

Jess stared at the message, her heart pounding. This was the third threatening message she had received today, and the pattern was becoming disturbingly clear. Someone was watching her every move, and their intentions were far from benign. She knew she had to continue her investigation, but the fear of what she might uncover was starting to weigh heavily on her.

Determined to push through her fear, Jess decided to visit her family the following day. Their recent behavior had been odd, and she needed to understand what was going on behind closed doors. She couldn't ignore the feeling that her family was somehow involved in this tangled web of deception. The financial troubles her father had mentioned and the strange distance from her mother only added to her concerns.

Jess arrived at her family's home the next afternoon, trying to keep her emotions in check. The house was quiet, and her parents were nowhere to be seen. She took a deep breath, steeling herself for what lay ahead. Her mother had always been the rock of the family, but recently, Jess had noticed a troubling shift in her demeanor. It was as if the warmth and affection she once relied on were now tinged with something darker and more elusive.

She found her mother in the kitchen, sitting at the table with a cup of tea. Her mother's face lit up with a strained smile as she saw Jess walk in. "Jess, dear. It's so good to see you."

Jess tried to return the smile, but her concern was evident. "Hi, Mom. Can we talk for a minute? I've been feeling like something's not right, and I need to understand what's going on."

Her mother's smile faltered slightly, but she nodded. "Of course. Let's sit down."

They took seats at the kitchen table, and Jess began to speak, choosing her words carefully. "I've been dealing with some strange situations lately. I've received threatening messages, and it's making me question everything and everyone around me. I need to know if there's something you're not telling me."

Her mother's eyes widened, and she looked down at her cup of tea, her hands trembling slightly. "Jess, I didn't want to worry you. There have been some financial issues, and your father and I have been trying to handle them on our own. We didn't want to add to your stress."

Jess's heart sank. She had hoped for a more concrete explanation, but her mother's vague response only deepened her unease. "I know about the financial problems, Mom. But there's something more going on here. It feels like there's a connection between our family issues and the threats I've been receiving."

Her mother looked pained. "Jess, I'm not sure what you're implying, but I can tell you that we've been trying to keep everything together. Your father has been under a lot of pressure, and it's affecting all of us."

Jess's frustration grew. "Mom, I need you to be honest with me. If there's something going on that could be putting us all at risk, I need to know. We're in this together, and keeping secrets isn't helping anyone."

Her mother took a deep breath, her eyes filling with tears. "I know you're right. There's been more to the financial troubles than we've let on. Your father made some poor decisions with investments, and it's put us in a difficult position. We've been trying to fix it, but we're struggling."

Jess's mind raced as she tried to process the information. The financial strain on her family could be a motive for someone to target them, but she still didn't understand the full picture. "Do you think this could be related to the threats I've been getting? Is there someone who might be using our financial problems against us?"

Her mother nodded slowly. "It's possible. There have been some unusual behaviors from people we thought we knew.

Your father might have been targeted by someone who knew about our situation."

Jess felt a pang of guilt. She had been so focused on her own troubles that she hadn't fully considered the impact on her family. "I need to figure out who might be behind this. If there's anyone who has a reason to harm us, I need to know."

Her mother wiped her eyes and nodded. "I understand. Just be careful, Jess. We're all feeling vulnerable right now."

With that, Jess left the kitchen and headed to her father's study. She found him sitting at his desk, buried in paperwork. His face was etched with worry, and he looked up with a weary expression as Jess entered.

"Hey, Dad," Jess said, trying to keep her voice steady. "I wanted to talk to you about something important."

Her father sighed and set his papers aside. "Sure, Jess. What's on your mind?"

Jess took a seat across from him and took a deep breath. "I've been receiving threatening messages lately, and they seem to be connected to some of the issues we're facing as a family. I need to understand what's really going on. Is there something you're not telling me?"

Her father's expression grew troubled. "Jess, I wish I could tell you everything, but it's complicated. We've been dealing with a lot, and I didn't want to burden you with it."

Jess's frustration boiled over. "Dad, if there's something that could be putting us at risk, I need to know. I can't keep pretending everything is fine when it clearly isn't."

Her father looked down, his shoulders slumping. "You're right. There's been more to our financial problems than we've let on. We've been targeted by some people who knew about our situation and took advantage of it."

Jess's heart raced. "Who are these people? What do they want from us?"

Her father shook his head. "I don't have all the answers. We've been trying to handle it privately, but it seems like someone is using our situation to their advantage. I didn't want to involve you in this, but it's clear now that it's affecting you too."

Jess felt a mix of anger and desperation. "I need to know who's behind this. If there's anyone who's threatening us, I need to find out before things get worse."

Her father nodded. "I'll try to dig up more information and see if I can find out who might be responsible. But you need to be careful. This situation is more dangerous than we realized."

As Jess left her father's study, she felt a renewed sense of urgency. The pieces of the puzzle were falling into place, but she still had a lot to uncover. The connection between her family's financial troubles and the threats she was receiving was becoming clearer, but the full extent of the danger remained unknown.

Her investigation led her to think about her recent interactions with her friends and acquaintances. Rachel's admission about the threats she had received and her nervous behavior were starting to make more sense. Jess knew she needed to reexamine her social circle to see if there were any other connections she had missed.

That evening, Jess decided to reach out to her old friend Daniel, who had been a reliable ally in the past. She needed someone who could offer a fresh perspective and help her navigate the complexities of her current situation.

She sent Daniel a message, asking if he could meet her the following day. To her relief, he agreed, and they arranged to meet at a local café.

The next day, Jess arrived at the café early, her mind racing with thoughts of her investigation. She had been up all night reviewing her social media posts and trying to connect the dots between the threats and her personal relationships. The café was a cozy spot, and Jess hoped the change of scenery would help her clear her head.

When Daniel arrived, he greeted Jess with a warm smile. "Hey, Jess. It's been a while. What's going on?"

Jess gave him a tight smile and gestured for him to sit. "Hi, Daniel. Thanks for meeting me. I'm dealing with some serious issues right now, and I need your help."

Daniel's expression grew serious. "Sure, what's up?"

Jess took a deep breath and began to explain the situation. She described the threatening messages, the strange behavior from her family, and her concerns about the connections between these events. Daniel listened intently, his brow furrowing as he absorbed the information.

"This is a lot to take in," Daniel said after Jess finished. "But it sounds like you're dealing with something much bigger than just a few pranks or random threats."

Jess nodded. "That's what I'm afraid of. I've been trying to piece everything together, but it feels like I'm missing something important. I need someone who can help me think through this and maybe find some leads I haven't considered."

Daniel thought for a moment. "Okay, I'll help however I can. Let's start by reviewing the messages and any other evidence you have. Maybe we can find something that points us in the right direction."

As they worked together, Jess felt a glimmer of hope. Having Daniel's support and perspective was a welcome relief in the midst of her turmoil. She knew that uncovering the truth would be challenging, but with a trusted friend by her side, she felt more equipped to face the storm ahead.

The investigation was far from over, and Jess's path was fraught with uncertainty. But she was determined to uncover the truth, no matter where it led her. The facades of her seemingly perfect life were crumbling, revealing hidden layers of deception and danger. Jess was ready to confront whatever lay ahead, armed with newfound resolve and the support of those who truly cared.

Chapter 5: Hidden Agendas

Jess sat in her room, phone in hand, staring at the string of cryptic messages that had slowly eroded her sense of control. The words blinked back at her, ominous and filled with threats that made her stomach churn. Each message tugged at a different corner of her life—an insecurity, a mistake, a secret. There was no one to trust, and everywhere she turned, the walls seemed to close in. As she scrolled through her latest post, which had quickly racked up hundreds of thousands of likes, Jess felt a bitter pang. The adoration felt hollow, the comments devoid of any meaning when she knew the truth behind her perfectly curated facade was unraveling.

Rachel had always been by her side, the steady friend who knew all the behind-the-scenes moments that never made it to Instagram. Jess had assumed that her fame, her constant pursuit of perfection, hadn't bothered Rachel. But last night, she had learned the truth.

"I was jealous," Rachel had confessed, her voice cracking with emotion. Jess could still hear the desperation in her words, still see the guilt etched across her best friend's face. "I didn't mean for it to get this far, I swear! I was angry, Jess, and you had everything—millions of followers, a perfect life. It just... it just got to me."

Jess had stared at her, stunned, trying to process what Rachel was saying. The messages, the threats, the creepy posts appearing on her accounts—Rachel had started them. She had been behind the initial wave of fear that had engulfed Jess's life. But as Jess listened, Rachel insisted it wasn't her who had escalated things. Someone else had taken the baton and run with it, far beyond what Rachel could control.

The words replayed in Jess's mind as she sat on her bed now, the morning light streaming through her window. How had her life spiraled into this nightmare? She could barely remember when things had been normal—before every notification became a jarring reminder of how fragile her world had become.

A soft knock at her door pulled her from her thoughts. "Jess?" It was her mother's voice, muffled but gentle, as if she knew something was deeply wrong but didn't want to intrude too much.

Jess cleared her throat. "Yeah?"

The door cracked open, and her mother peeked in, offering a cautious smile. "I made breakfast if you're hungry."

"I'm not really in the mood, Mom," Jess replied, not moving from her spot. She didn't have the energy to pretend everything was okay right now.

Her mom stepped in fully, her concern evident in the way she hovered near the door, unsure whether to approach or leave her daughter alone. "Jess, you've been... distant lately. Is everything alright? I mean, I know with your career and all, there's a lot of pressure, but if something else is going on, I'm here for you."

Jess forced a smile, but it didn't reach her eyes. "I'm fine, just a lot going on with the brand deals and posts, you know?"

Her mother's expression didn't change, the worry still etched across her face. Jess knew that wasn't enough to convince her, but she didn't have the strength to explain everything. How could she even begin to unpack the layers of lies, the pressure, and the threats without unraveling completely?

"I'll come down in a bit," Jess added, hoping to cut the conversation short. Her mom lingered for a moment longer, then finally nodded and left, pulling the door closed behind her.

Jess exhaled, rubbing her temples. The truth was, she couldn't keep living like this. The perfect image she had crafted online was cracking, and now even her closest friend had admitted to trying to tear her down from the inside. And yet, despite Rachel's confession, something about her story didn't sit right. Rachel was petty sometimes, sure, but could jealousy have driven her to orchestrate a campaign to destroy Jess's life? It felt too calculated, too sinister for someone as unambitious as Rachel.

Her phone buzzed again, and Jess tensed. She hesitated before glancing at the screen. Another message.

You can't trust anyone, Jess. Even the people closest to you have their own agenda. It's not over yet.

Jess felt her stomach twist. The account was still anonymous, a mixture of numbers and letters, but the message felt personal. More personal than Rachel's confessions ever had. It was like whoever was sending these knew Jess intimately, understood her fears and vulnerabilities in a way that made her feel exposed and naked.

The thought of Rachel played in the back of her mind. She had confessed to being jealous, but had she really stopped? Could she still be behind all this? Jess's mind raced as she considered the possibility. She needed to confront Rachel again—find out if there was more she wasn't telling.

With a surge of determination, Jess grabbed her phone and called Rachel. The phone rang and rang before finally going to voicemail. Jess bit her lip, irritation creeping in. She texted her instead:

We need to talk. Meet me at the coffee shop near school in an hour.

She tossed the phone on her bed and began pacing her room, her nerves on edge. Rachel had a lot more explaining to do. Jess wasn't going to let her off that easily. If she was still lying, Jess needed to know. There was too much at stake.

An hour later, Jess sat at the small table by the window of the café, tapping her fingers anxiously on the table. The smell of roasted coffee filled the air, but Jess barely noticed. She kept her eyes glued to the door, waiting for Rachel to show up. She was running late, and Jess's patience was wearing thin.

Finally, the door swung open, and Rachel walked in. Her usual laid-back demeanor seemed a little more nervous today—her eyes darting around the room before settling on Jess. She walked over and sat down without a word, fidgeting with her phone.

"Hey," Jess said coolly, crossing her arms. "You're late."

Rachel looked sheepish. "Sorry, I... I wasn't sure if I should come."

"You think after what you told me last night, you can just not show up?" Jess's voice was sharp, frustration bubbling to the surface.

Rachel sighed, avoiding Jess's gaze. "I get it, okay? You're mad. But I already told you everything. I didn't mean for any of this to happen."

Jess leaned forward, narrowing her eyes. "You said you didn't mean for this to happen, but how do I know you're telling the truth? You've already lied to me, Rachel. How do I know you're not still lying?"

Rachel's face flushed. "I'm not! I swear, Jess, I only did the first few messages. I wanted to scare you, that's all. I thought maybe you'd get knocked down a peg or two, and then I'd stop. But then the messages started coming from someone else, and I couldn't control it anymore!"

Jess's eyes bore into her friend's, searching for any hint of deception. "Who? Who would do this, Rachel?"

"I don't know!" Rachel insisted, her voice rising. "I've been trying to figure it out, but I don't have any answers. I never wanted this to get so serious, Jess. I never wanted to hurt you."

Jess clenched her fists under the table, her anger simmering just below the surface. She wanted to believe Rachel, but something still felt off. "Do you realize what you've done? My entire life is falling apart because of this, Rachel. And you think just saying sorry is enough?"

Rachel's lip trembled, and for a moment, Jess thought she might cry. "I know, Jess. I'm sorry. I've been losing sleep over this. I've been getting messages too, but I don't know who's behind them."

"You're getting messages?" Jess's eyebrows shot up in surprise. "Why didn't you tell me?"

"Because I thought you wouldn't believe me. After all, I'm the one who started this mess." Rachel wiped at her eyes, sniffling. "I just didn't know what to do."

Jess sat back, her mind whirling. If Rachel was telling the truth, then there was someone else—someone who had picked up where Rachel left off and was determined to destroy Jess's life. But who?

"Rachel, I need you to be completely honest with me from now on," Jess said, her voice softer but still firm. "I can't do this alone. If you're really sorry, then you need to help me figure out who's doing this."

Rachel nodded vigorously. "I will, Jess. I'll do whatever it takes to fix this."

Jess wasn't sure if she fully trusted Rachel yet, but for now, she didn't have much choice. She needed allies, and Rachel—despite everything—was one of the few people who knew just how deep this nightmare went.

Jess's phone buzzed on the table, pulling her attention away from Rachel. She glanced down and saw another message from the anonymous account. Her heart skipped a beat as she read the words.

You think you're getting closer, but you're not. This is far from over.

Her breath caught in her throat as the weight of the message settled over her. Whoever was behind this wasn't done playing their twisted game. And Jess was no closer to figuring out who it was.

"We need to find out who's behind this, fast," Jess said, her voice tight with urgency.

Rachel nodded. "But how? They're hiding behind an anonymous account."

Jess stared at the message, her mind racing. "There has to be a way to trace it. We need to find someone who knows how."

And with that, the next phase of their plan began to take shape—a plan to unmask the person who was tearing Jess's life apart, one lie at a time.

Jess sat on the edge of her bed, her thoughts swirling. The revelation that Rachel had been the one behind the initial threats still stung, but even more troubling was her insistence that she wasn't responsible for the current messages. Rachel's apology had been tearful and full of regret, but Jess couldn't shake the feeling that there was more to the story. After all, the messages had escalated—becoming more personal, more dangerous—and Rachel didn't seem like the type to orchestrate something so sinister on her own.

Jess opened her laptop and stared at the screen, her eyes scanning over the endless stream of comments, likes, and reposts flooding her social media accounts. Despite her management's advice to stay silent, she couldn't just let it go. The messages had to be coming from someone who knew her—someone who knew more than they should.

Her gaze fell on an old photo, one from a few years ago. It was her, Rachel, and Amanda. They'd been inseparable once, before Amanda's jealousy turned their friendship into bitter rivalry. Jess frowned. Could Amanda have been behind this all along?

The thought nagged at her, refusing to let go. Amanda had always been ruthless, always seeking attention. She'd built her own following by riding on Jess's coattails, then trashing her when their friendship fell apart. Jess had long suspected Amanda of spreading rumors about her in the past, but this—this was on another level.

Jess pulled up Amanda's social media profile. It was full of the usual carefully curated shots—lavish trips, designer outfits, flawless makeup. But something felt off. Jess clicked through the posts, her eyes narrowing as she spotted a subtle pattern. Amanda had been making vague references to someone's "fall from grace" for weeks now. The timing lined up perfectly with the start of the anonymous messages Jess had been receiving.

Jess's stomach churned. Could Amanda really be doing this? Would she go as far as to ruin Jess's life just for the sake of clicks and followers?

She needed proof.

The next morning, Jess sat at a small coffee shop downtown, her fingers tapping nervously on the table. Across from her, Daniel—a tech-savvy friend she'd met through mutual acquaintances—was hunched over his laptop, typing furiously.

"I'm telling you," Jess said, her voice a hushed whisper. "Amanda's behind this. I just need something—anything—to prove it."

Daniel glanced up from his screen. "If she's smart, she'll be using fake accounts, VPNs, anything to cover her tracks."

Jess sighed, sinking deeper into her chair. "I know, but there has to be something. I can't let her get away with this."

Daniel gave her a reassuring smile. "We'll find something."

Minutes turned into hours as Daniel dug deeper into the web of messages and posts. He was meticulous, tracing IP addresses, cross-referencing timestamps, and searching for any connection that could link Amanda to the threats. Jess watched anxiously, her heart racing every time Daniel paused to inspect something.

Finally, he leaned back in his chair, a triumphant look on his face.

"I think I found something," he said, spinning the laptop around for Jess to see. "Check this out."

On the screen was a list of anonymous accounts, each one connected to posts that had either threatened Jess or hinted at her involvement in the local crimes. Daniel had managed to trace the accounts back to a shared IP address.

Jess's eyes widened. "That's Amanda's address, isn't it?"

Daniel nodded. "It's a match. Whoever is behind these accounts is using Amanda's internet connection."

A mix of relief and fury washed over Jess. She finally had the proof she needed. Amanda had gone too far this time, and Jess wasn't going to let her destroy everything she'd worked for.

But as Jess stared at the screen, something else caught her attention. One of the anonymous accounts had been active long before the messages started. In fact, it had been posting subtle jabs at Jess for months, even before Amanda and Jess's friendship had dissolved.

"That's weird," Jess muttered, pointing to the screen. "Why would Amanda have been targeting me so long ago?"

Daniel frowned, leaning in for a closer look. "It doesn't add up," he agreed. "Amanda's always been competitive, but this level of obsession—it seems personal."

Jess felt a chill run down her spine. Could there be someone else involved? Someone who had been feeding Amanda information, stoking her jealousy, and pushing her to act?

As she sat there, Jess's mind raced back to a conversation she'd had with her father months ago. He'd warned her about trusting too many people, especially in the influencer world, where everyone had their own hidden agendas. At the time, she'd brushed off his concerns, convinced that she knew who her real friends were. But now, with everything unraveling, she wasn't so sure.

"I need to talk to her," Jess said, her voice firm.

Daniel raised an eyebrow. "Amanda? Are you sure that's a good idea? She's clearly unhinged."

Jess shook her head. "No, I need to confront her. If she's behind this, I want to see her reaction. And if she's not... then I need to find out who is."

That afternoon, Jess found herself standing outside Amanda's high-rise apartment, her heart pounding in her chest. She'd texted Amanda earlier, asking to talk, and to her surprise, Amanda had agreed without hesitation.

As Jess rode the elevator to the top floor, she rehearsed what she was going to say. She needed to keep her cool, stay in control. Amanda was manipulative, and Jess knew that one wrong move could set her off. But she also couldn't afford to be passive anymore. This had gone too far.

The elevator doors slid open, and Jess stepped out onto the marble floor of Amanda's lavish penthouse. She knocked on the door, her hands trembling slightly. Moments later, Amanda appeared, her face lighting up in a perfect, practiced smile.

"Jess," Amanda greeted her, stepping aside to let her in. "It's been a while."

Jess forced a tight smile, walking into the apartment. The place was just as over-the-top as Amanda's online persona—modern, sleek, filled with expensive furniture and art. Everything about it screamed success, but to Jess, it felt hollow.

"I'm not here to catch up," Jess said, her voice steady despite the nervousness bubbling inside her.

Amanda arched an eyebrow, closing the door behind her. "Oh? Then what brings you to my humble abode?"

Jess took a deep breath. "I know it was you, Amanda. The messages, the lies—you've been trying to ruin my life."

Amanda blinked, her expression unreadable for a moment. Then, to Jess's surprise, she laughed. It wasn't the kind of laugh you shared with a friend—it was cold, sharp, and full of malice.

"You think I did all that?" Amanda asked, crossing her arms. "Please, Jess. I'm flattered that you think I'm capable of such a grand scheme, but you give me too much credit."

Jess's fists clenched at her sides. "Don't play dumb. I have proof. Daniel traced the accounts back to your IP address."

Amanda's eyes narrowed, but she didn't lose her composure. Instead, she shrugged, walking over to the massive floor-to-ceiling windows that overlooked the city.

"Maybe I posted a few things here and there," she admitted, her voice casual. "But I didn't do anything illegal. All I did was show people the real you. The girl behind the perfect filter."

Jess felt her blood boil. "The real me? You've been framing me for crimes I didn't commit!"

Amanda turned to face her, her expression hardening. "I didn't frame you, Jess. I just let people see the cracks in your perfect little image. You built your empire on lies, and now it's falling apart. I just gave it a little push."

Jess's mind raced. Amanda was admitting to manipulating her image, but something about her tone made Jess pause. There was more to this. Amanda was vindictive, yes, but this felt too calculated, too well-orchestrated for Amanda to have done it all alone.

"A little push?" Jess repeated, her voice cold. "Or was someone else pulling the strings?"

Amanda's smile faltered for the first time, and Jess saw a flicker of uncertainty in her eyes.

"I don't know what you're talking about," Amanda said quickly, but her voice lacked the confidence it had moments ago.

Jess stepped forward, her heart pounding. "You're not working alone, are you? Someone else has been feeding you information, pushing you to do this."

Amanda hesitated, and for a brief moment, Jess thought she might confess. But then Amanda's face hardened again, and she shook her head.

"Believe what you want," Amanda said, her voice low. "But you're the one who let this happen. You're the one who built your entire life on likes and lies. And now you're paying the price."

Jess felt a lump form in her throat, but she refused to let Amanda see her cry. Without another word, she turned on her heel and stormed out of the apartment, her mind spinning with everything she'd just heard.

As she rode the elevator down to the street, Jess's phone buzzed in her pocket. She pulled it out and glanced at the screen. It was another anonymous message, this one more chilling than the rest.

"You're getting closer, Jess. But you're not ready for the truth."

Jess's heart raced as she stared at the words. Whoever was behind this wasn't done yet. And she had a feeling that the real game was just beginning.

Chapter 6: The Rival's Plot

Jess Turner sat at the edge of her bed, staring at her phone with a sense of dread creeping up her spine. Her once pristine Instagram feed was now tainted by a growing number of accusatory comments and posts from people who had once idolized her. The perfectly curated world she'd spent years building was now unraveling at the seams. The anonymous messages, the cryptic posts, the constant barrage of threats—all of it had culminated in the most gut-wrenching revelation yet: Amanda.

Amanda Lawson. The girl who had once been Jess's best friend, before the fallouts, the jealousy, the vicious competition. Amanda, who had now apparently devoted herself to ruining Jess's life. And she was succeeding.

Jess swiped through her notifications with trembling fingers. Comments flooded her posts, each one a knife in her heart.

"I can't believe you would do something like that."

"How could you lie to all of us?"

"I thought you were different, Jess. Guess I was wrong."

Her public image was in tatters. The accusations were vague but damaging. Crimes? Involvement in shady dealings? Jess didn't even know where the lies began or ended anymore. But Amanda had planted seeds of doubt, carefully curating her own narrative to paint Jess as a villain. And Jess had unknowingly played right into her hands.

She closed her phone, her chest tightening as she leaned back against the headboard. Her eyes wandered to the framed photos on her dresser—images of her with her family, her friends, and even Amanda. There they were, frozen in time, smiling together as if nothing could break them apart. Jess grimaced at the sight. It had been naïve of her to think they would stay friends forever. The influencer world wasn't built for lasting bonds. Everyone wanted to be on top. And Amanda, apparently, wanted that more than anyone else.

Her mind raced as she recalled the pieces of information she had gathered over the past few days. The anonymous account that had been sending her threats wasn't just a random troll. No, it had been orchestrated, manipulated by Amanda. The realization hit Jess like a brick. All of Amanda's actions had been calculated—from the cryptic posts to the fake evidence pointing to Jess's supposed criminal involvement.

Jess had already confronted Rachel about the initial threats. Rachel had admitted to her part, driven by jealousy and the desire to bring Jess down a peg. But even Rachel, as guilty as she was, didn't seem to be behind the current mess. This was Amanda's doing. Amanda had somehow twisted the narrative to fit her own goals, using Rachel as an unwitting pawn in her larger game.

Jess stood up from the bed, pacing the room as her thoughts spiraled. She had to figure out Amanda's endgame. What was she really after? Fame? Power? Or was it just revenge for the falling out they'd had years ago?

Jess grabbed her laptop and sat down at her desk, determined to uncover more. She started with Amanda's social media profiles, combing through her posts and comments. On the surface, Amanda's accounts were as polished as ever—images of her living her best life, collaborating with brands, attending exclusive events. But something was off. The captions, the timing of her posts, the comments from Amanda's followers... They all seemed too perfect, too orchestrated.

It didn't take long for Jess to find what she was looking for. A series of posts from Amanda's account, posted around the same time the accusations against Jess had started. The captions were subtle but laced with innuendo:

"Some people will do anything for fame, even if it means crossing the line."

"Be careful who you trust. Not everyone is as innocent as they seem."

Jess's stomach churned. Amanda had been planting doubts in her followers' minds for weeks, maybe even months, setting the stage for the scandal that was now unraveling before Jess's eyes. And her followers had eaten it up, believing every word without question.

Jess leaned back in her chair, her heart pounding in her chest. She couldn't sit back and let Amanda destroy her reputation. She had to fight back, but how? Amanda was always one step ahead, and Jess felt like she was constantly playing catch-up.

Her phone buzzed on the desk, pulling her from her thoughts. A new message, from the anonymous account.

You're running out of time, Jess. Tell the truth, or I will.

Jess's pulse quickened as she stared at the message. She didn't know what truth the person was referring to. There was nothing to confess—she hadn't committed any crimes, hadn't done anything wrong. But whoever was behind this wanted to paint a different story, and the world was starting to believe them.

Jess's thoughts turned to her family. Her father had been acting strange lately—distant, distracted, as if something was weighing heavily on him. Jess had noticed the change, but she hadn't had the energy to confront him about it. Her mother, too, had been keeping secrets. Jess could feel it. They were both hiding something, and Jess couldn't shake the feeling that it was connected to Amanda's scheme.

She needed answers, and she needed them now.

Grabbing her jacket, Jess stormed out of her room and down the stairs, her mind racing with questions. Her father was in his office, the door slightly ajar. She hesitated for a moment before pushing it open.

"Dad," she said, her voice trembling with a mixture of anger and fear. "We need to talk."

Her father looked up from his desk, his expression unreadable. He didn't say anything, just gestured for her to sit down. Jess crossed the room and sat in the chair opposite him, her heart pounding in her chest.

"What's going on?" she demanded. "You've been acting strange for weeks, and I know it's connected to what's happening to me. Amanda is trying to destroy my life, and I need to know if you're involved in any of this."

Her father's face paled, and for a moment, Jess thought he might deny it. But then he sighed heavily and leaned back in his chair, rubbing his temples.

"I didn't want to involve you in this, Jess," he said quietly. "But I think it's time you knew the truth."

Jess's stomach twisted in knots. "What truth?"

Her father looked at her, his eyes filled with regret. "It's about Amanda. And your mother."

Jess's breath caught in her throat. "What does Mom have to do with this?"

Her father hesitated before speaking, as if weighing the consequences of his words. "Your mother and Amanda's family have a... history. A financial history. Years ago, before you and Amanda were even friends, there was a business deal gone wrong. Your mother and Amanda's father were involved in a joint venture, and things didn't end well. There were accusations of fraud, lawsuits... It was a mess. And your mother... well, she wasn't exactly innocent in all of it."

Jess stared at her father in disbelief. "What are you saying?"

"I'm saying that Amanda's hatred for you isn't just about your falling out as friends," her father said, his voice heavy with guilt. "It's about revenge. Revenge for what happened between our families."

Jess's mind reeled. She had always thought Amanda's grudge stemmed from their personal issues—the competition, the jealousy, the betrayals. But this was so much bigger than that. This was about their families, about old wounds and long-held grudges that had festered over the years.

"Amanda blames your mother for what happened to her family," her father continued. "And now she's using this scandal to get back at both of you. She's trying to ruin your life as payback for what she believes your mother did to hers."

Jess's hands trembled as she processed the revelation. "Why didn't you tell me this sooner?" she demanded. "Why didn't Mom tell me?"

"We didn't want to burden you with our mistakes," her father said, his voice barely above a whisper. "We thought it was in the past, that it wouldn't affect you. But clearly, we were wrong."

Jess felt a surge of anger rise within her. Her parents had kept this from her, and now she was paying the price. Amanda's attacks weren't just personal—they were part of a calculated plan to destroy her entire family.

"What am I supposed to do now?" Jess asked, her voice trembling. "How do I stop her?"

Her father looked at her with a mixture of sadness and determination. "You have to fight back, Jess. You have to expose the truth, not just about what Amanda's doing to you, but about what happened between our families. It's the only way to clear your name."

Jess nodded, her mind racing with the possibilities. She couldn't let Amanda win. She had to find a way to turn the tide, to expose Amanda's lies before it was too late.

But as Jess stood up to leave, a thought crossed her mind—a chilling realization that made her heart stop.

What if Amanda wasn't working alone?

The anonymous messages, the cryptic posts... They couldn't all be Amanda. There was someone else pulling the strings, someone who had been orchestrating this from the shadows.

And Jess had no idea who it was.

As she left her father's office, a sense of dread settled over her. She was running out of time, and the walls were closing in.

But Jess Turner wasn't going down without a fight.

She would uncover the truth, no matter how deep the lies ran.

The weight of the discovery Jess had made felt suffocating as she sat in front of her computer, Amanda's fabricated narrative about her spinning out of control online. Every hour, it seemed, a new piece of "evidence" against Jess appeared in a different corner of the internet. Comments flooded her social media posts, her direct messages were filled with hate, and hashtags that questioned her integrity and involvement in criminal activities were trending globally.

Jess had no idea how Amanda had managed to create such a web of deceit so quickly. The planted screenshots, the doctored images, the conversations Jess never had — it was overwhelming. Amanda was using her skills in the social media world not only to tear Jess down but to turn her followers against her. She had been meticulous in her plan, ensuring that each new accusation felt more authentic than the last. Jess could see the narrative Amanda was weaving, framing her as not just an irresponsible influencer but as someone with deeply immoral intentions.

Jess's efforts to expose Amanda were met with immediate resistance. Every attempt she made to post a defense or clarify the situation was drowned out by a flood of angry comments. It was as though Amanda had anticipated every step Jess would take. When Jess would try to clear up one accusation, Amanda would release another piece of false information — something even more shocking than the last. Jess's every move felt trapped in a digital cage that Amanda had built.

Sitting back from her desk, Jess looked at her phone, her heart racing as notifications continued to flood in. She had tried to release a statement earlier, a video explaining the situation and warning her followers about Amanda's lies. But Amanda was clever. Almost immediately after Jess posted, Amanda had countered by leaking more fake messages and screenshots, making Jess's explanation seem like a weak, disingenuous attempt at damage control.

Scrolling through her timeline, Jess saw the pattern of lies stretching before her, intricate and calculated. Comments ranged from shocked disbelief to outright condemnation, and what hurt the most was that some of these were from people who had been her supporters for years. It felt like she was losing everything, piece by piece.

"How do you even fight something like this?" Jess muttered to herself, feeling helpless. Amanda wasn't just attacking her brand or reputation — she was tearing apart the life Jess had built. All the trust Jess had worked so hard to earn with her audience was now hanging by a thread, all because of this manipulative, deeply personal vendetta.

In frustration, Jess slammed her laptop shut, feeling trapped by her own inability to counter Amanda's lies fast enough. Amanda had become a master puppeteer, pulling the strings on this carefully orchestrated takedown, and Jess was left scrambling to cut those strings before her entire life unraveled.

Jess knew she needed to regroup and approach this differently. Continuing to defend herself in the same way wasn't working. The more she posted in her own defense, the more Amanda had ammunition to make her seem guilty or complicit. It was like a vicious cycle, and Jess realized that she was being reactive instead of proactive.

A few hours later, Jess sat in the living room, staring blankly at the television. She hadn't turned it on, and the silence was deafening. Her mother came into the room, concern etched deeply on her face.

"Jess, sweetie, I don't know how much more of this you can take," her mother said, sitting down beside her. "Have you thought about talking to a lawyer? Maybe they can stop Amanda legally."

Jess shook her head. "I've thought about it, but the damage is already done online. Even if we sued Amanda, the court of public opinion has already made up its mind. She's winning. Everyone is seeing these fake messages and thinking I'm some kind of criminal."

Her mother reached out and squeezed her hand. "You're not a criminal, Jess. People who truly know you won't believe it."

"But that's the thing, Mom," Jess said bitterly. "Most of my followers don't really know me. They know the image I've put out there. The curated version. And Amanda is twisting that image into something I barely recognize. Right now, they believe her more than they believe me."

Jess stood and began pacing the room, her mind racing. "I need to get ahead of her. I need to find a way to make people see the truth before she completely destroys my credibility. If I can prove she's behind all of this, then maybe I have a chance."

Her mother frowned. "And how do you plan to do that? She's been careful, hasn't she? Covering her tracks?"

Jess stopped and faced her mother. "Yes, but there's always something. No one's perfect, not even Amanda. I just need to figure out where she slipped up."

Her mother hesitated before speaking. "Be careful, Jess. She's already taken so much from you. Don't let her take any more."

That night, Jess couldn't sleep. Every time she closed her eyes, all she could see were the hateful comments, the accusations piling up against her. Her mind kept going back to one thing: Amanda's need to be perfect. She'd always been like that, even when they were still friends. Amanda never left any room for mistakes, and she had a reputation for being ruthlessly strategic. But Jess knew that sometimes, the need to be perfect could also lead to carelessness.

Sitting up in bed, Jess grabbed her phone. There had to be something, some small clue that could link Amanda to the fake accounts and false evidence. She opened Instagram and scrolled through Amanda's recent posts, trying to look beyond the surface-level perfection of Amanda's carefully curated images. Each post looked like it belonged in a glossy magazine, but Jess knew that beneath the surface, there had to be cracks in the façade. Everyone had them — Amanda included.

As she studied the photos, Jess noticed something strange. Amanda had posted a photo a few days ago at the same time one of the anonymous threats against Jess had been posted. In the photo, Amanda was smiling in front of a sunset, holding a glass of champagne, looking effortlessly elegant. But something about the timestamp and location felt off. Jess knew Amanda lived hours away from the location she claimed to be at in the post. It wasn't a huge detail, but it was enough to make Jess wonder if Amanda had doctored not just her accusations but her own posts to create alibis.

If Jess could prove that Amanda wasn't where she claimed to be when certain posts went live, it might be enough to raise doubts about Amanda's credibility. It wasn't a smoking gun, but it was something. Jess quickly screenshot the post and saved it to her phone.

The next morning, Jess took her laptop to a local café, a quiet spot where she could think clearly. She didn't want to be at home, surrounded by the reminders of the chaos Amanda had caused. As she settled into her seat and opened her laptop, she began sifting through Amanda's social media profiles, looking for any inconsistencies.

After hours of searching, Jess found another potential clue: a series of comments Amanda had left on an influencer forum. They weren't tied directly to Amanda's account but had been posted by an anonymous user. However, the writing style and certain phrases were unmistakably Amanda's. One of the comments discussed how easy it was to manipulate followers with "a little creativity and the right resources." Jess's pulse quickened. The comments were from a few months ago, long before Amanda had started her current campaign against Jess, but they revealed Amanda's mindset and her willingness to manipulate others online.

Jess took screenshots of the forum thread, carefully cataloging everything she found. It wasn't a confession, but it was a piece of the puzzle — another crack in Amanda's perfectly constructed image.

By the time Jess left the café, she felt a glimmer of hope. For the first time in days, she felt like she had a chance to fight back. Amanda wasn't invincible, and if Jess could find more evidence like this, she could start to turn the tide.

But as soon as she walked through her front door, her phone buzzed with a new notification. Another message from the anonymous account.

"You think you're smart, don't you? You'll never win this game. Give up while you still can."

Jess's heart sank. It was like Amanda could sense her every move. Jess knew she was being watched, manipulated at every step, but the message only steeled her resolve. Amanda wanted her to give up, but Jess wasn't going to back down — not now.

She had spent too long running from the lies. Now it was time to face them head-on, no matter the cost.

Jess sat down at her desk and began drafting a new video statement. This time, she wouldn't just defend herself. She would start to expose Amanda, piece by piece. It was a risk — Amanda would likely retaliate even harder — but Jess had no other choice.

As she filmed herself, she felt a sense of determination rising within her. The fight wasn't over yet, and Jess was ready to take back control of her life. She wouldn't let Amanda's lies destroy her.

The public might not believe her immediately, but she was done playing the victim. This time, Jess was going to fight. And she would make sure the truth came out, no matter how hard Amanda tried to bury it.

Chapter 7: Fractured Trust

The afternoon sun filtered through the half-drawn curtains, casting a muted glow on Jess's room. She lay sprawled on her bed, staring blankly at her phone, its screen glowing with the stream of hateful comments and allegations flooding her social media. The public backlash from Amanda's manipulations had spiraled out of control, and Jess was barely holding herself together. The pristine image she had worked so hard to build was disintegrating, piece by piece, and with it, her sense of control.

Her fingers hovered over her mother's number, hesitant to dial. Jess's mind was still reeling from the discoveries of the past few days: Amanda's scheme, Rachel's betrayal, and the growing suspicion that her family might be hiding more than she'd ever imagined. Her mother, usually a rock of support, had been strangely distant lately. The tension at home had been palpable, and Jess couldn't shake the feeling that her parents knew more about the situation than they were letting on.

With a deep breath, Jess pressed the call button, heart racing as it rang. After what felt like an eternity, her mother picked up.

"Jess?" her mother's voice sounded strained, a far cry from the warmth Jess was used to.

"Mom, can we talk?" Jess's voice cracked, unable to conceal the emotional weight she was carrying.

A pause followed, long enough to make Jess's anxiety spike. "Of course, sweetie," her mother finally replied. "What's on your mind?"

Jess sat up, gripping the phone tighter. "Mom, I need to know the truth. About Amanda, about everything. I feel like... there's something you're not telling me."

The silence on the other end of the line was deafening, and for a brief moment, Jess thought her mother had hung up. Then, her mother let out a heavy sigh, one that carried years of guilt and unspoken truths.

"Jess, I—" her mother started, then stopped. Jess could hear her struggling to find the words, which only heightened her fear. "I never wanted you to be involved in any of this. I thought I could protect you, but... I guess I was wrong."

Jess's chest tightened. She hadn't expected her mother to admit so much, so quickly. "Involved in what?" Jess's voice was sharp, demanding answers.

"I've known about Amanda for a while now," her mother confessed, her voice barely above a whisper. "I found out she was planning something, but I didn't think it would go this far. I didn't think she'd actually do this to you."

Jess felt her heart plummet into her stomach. Her hands trembled, her knuckles turning white as she clutched the phone. "You knew? And you didn't say anything?" she asked, her voice laced with disbelief.

"I didn't know how to tell you, Jess," her mother's voice broke, filled with remorse. "I thought if I intervened, it would make things worse. I didn't want to risk your career, your life—"

"My life is falling apart, Mom!" Jess cried, her frustration boiling over. "You should have told me. How could you let this happen?"

Her mother's sobs were faint on the other end. Jess closed her eyes, fighting back tears of her own. The woman who had always been her source of strength now seemed weak, her silence inexcusable. Jess felt betrayed, not just by Amanda and Rachel, but by the one person she thought she could always count on.

"I was scared," her mother whispered. "I was scared for you, and for us."

Jess's mind raced. The pressure, the lies, the secrets—it was all crashing down around her, and she wasn't sure how to make sense of any of it. Her mother's confession had shaken her to her core. If her own family had been hiding things from her, what else was lurking in the shadows?

"I need to know everything," Jess demanded. "Why would Amanda do this? And what else are you hiding from me?"

Another long pause followed. Jess braced herself, knowing that whatever came next would only deepen the wounds that had already been inflicted.

"Amanda and I... we used to be friends, Jess," her mother admitted. "Before you were born. We had a falling out—something that was never fully resolved. I thought it was in the past, but when you and Amanda became friends, she saw it as an opportunity to get back at me."

Jess's head spun as she processed the revelation. Amanda's vendetta wasn't just against her—it had roots that extended much deeper, into her family's past. This was personal, and Jess had been caught in the crossfire.

"Why didn't you warn me?" Jess asked, her voice barely audible.

"I didn't think she'd involve you like this," her mother said, her voice filled with regret. "I thought she was just jealous of your success, and I didn't want to stir up old wounds. I was wrong. I should have told you everything from the beginning."

Jess sat in stunned silence, the weight of her mother's words pressing down on her like a boulder. The web of lies and deceit that had been spun around her life felt more tangled than ever. Amanda's attack wasn't just about Jess's fame or reputation—it was part of a long-standing grudge that Jess had unknowingly walked into.

"Mom," Jess finally said, her voice shaky, "I need to know what else you're hiding. This isn't just about Amanda, is it?"

Her mother hesitated again, and Jess could practically hear her heart pounding in her chest as she waited for the next bombshell to drop.

"I don't know if I can tell you everything, not yet," her mother admitted. "But I'll tell you this: Amanda's not the only one who's been manipulating things. Your father—"

Jess's breath caught in her throat. "What about Dad?"

"I don't know all the details," her mother said quickly, as if trying to prevent Jess from jumping to conclusions. "But he's been acting strange lately, and I think it has something to do with Amanda's schemes. He's been keeping things from me too, Jess. I'm sorry. I didn't want you to be dragged into this, but I think... I think he's involved."

Jess felt like the ground had been ripped out from under her. Her father, who had always been so supportive and loving, was now another question mark in the growing mystery of her life. Nothing made sense anymore. How could her own parents have secrets like this?

"I'll find out what he's hiding," her mother added, her voice steely with determination. "We'll get to the bottom of this. But Jess, you have to be careful. Amanda's dangerous, and we don't know what else she's capable of."

Jess nodded, though her mother couldn't see her. "I will be," she whispered. "I just... I don't know who to trust anymore."

"I understand," her mother said softly. "But we'll figure this out together. I promise."

They hung up, and Jess sat in the heavy silence of her room, the weight of her mother's revelations settling over her like a thick fog. She had never felt so alone, so vulnerable. The people she had relied on her whole life were suddenly strangers, hiding things from her, keeping secrets that had the power to destroy everything she had worked for.

Her thoughts were interrupted by a knock on her door. Jess turned, startled, as her father poked his head in.

"Hey, sweetheart," he said, his tone unnervingly casual. "Everything okay?"

Jess swallowed hard, her mother's words ringing in her ears. She forced a smile, but it felt brittle on her face. "Yeah, Dad. Just... thinking."

He nodded, stepping into the room. "I know things have been tough lately. But we'll get through this, okay? We're a family. We stick together."

Jess stared at him, trying to reconcile the man she had always known with the person her mother had hinted at—someone with secrets, someone possibly involved in Amanda's schemes. The thought made her stomach churn.

"Yeah," Jess murmured, her voice hollow. "We'll get through it."

Her father smiled and patted her shoulder. "That's my girl. Stay strong, okay? And let me know if you need anything."

As he left the room, Jess's gaze followed him, her mind racing. What was he hiding? Could he really be involved in Amanda's plot? The doubts gnawed at her, making her question everything she had ever believed about her family.

She needed answers, but more than that, she needed to protect herself. If her own parents couldn't be trusted, who could?

Jess grabbed her phone and opened her messages, scrolling through the flood of hate and threats until she found Rachel's name. Her fingers hovered over the keyboard, unsure of what to say. Despite everything, part of her still wanted to believe that Rachel had told her the truth—that she wasn't part of the ongoing attacks. But after what she had just learned, trusting anyone felt impossible.

She tossed her phone onto the bed and buried her face in her hands, the weight of the situation pressing down on her. Every direction she turned, there were more lies, more secrets. The perfect life she had presented to the world was unraveling at the seams, and Jess wasn't sure how much more she could take.

But she couldn't give up. Not now. Not when the truth was so close, just out of reach. She would get to the bottom of this, no matter what it took.

She had to.

Jess sat on the edge of her bed, her phone clutched tightly in her hand. The blue glow of the screen cast sharp shadows on her face, highlighting the deep lines of stress that had begun to settle in, aging her young features. She stared at the unread message from her father, the words dancing on the screen, begging for her attention. He wanted to talk, but Jess didn't know if she had the strength to face him. Not after everything she'd uncovered, not after the secrets that had slowly unraveled her sense of security, leaving her feeling as if she were standing on a precipice, with nothing but betrayal beneath her.

Her mind was still spinning from her mother's confession. The idea that her mother had known about Amanda's schemes—had known and done nothing—was almost too much to bear. But that wasn't all. Jess couldn't shake the nagging feeling that her father was hiding something deeper. His recent behavior—the strange late-night phone calls, the odd absences—had gone from perplexing to suspicious.

She let out a shaky breath, tossing her phone aside and curling up in a ball, burying her face in her knees. What was happening to her life? Just a few weeks ago, she had been the girl everyone wanted to be—Jess Turner, social media queen, with millions of followers hanging on her every post. Her world had been one of filters and carefully constructed perfection, where every angle was curated and every moment made to appear effortless. But it was all a lie, wasn't it? Every like, every heart emoji—it was all built on a foundation of dishonesty and manipulation.

The door creaked open slightly, and Jess's father poked his head inside. "Can I come in?" His voice was softer than usual, as though he knew the fragility of the moment. She didn't answer right away. Instead, she remained silent, staring at the space in front of her, unsure of how to respond.

"Jess," he tried again, stepping fully into the room now. "We need to talk. Please."

She still didn't look up, but her body tensed at the sound of his footsteps approaching. When he finally sat down next to her, she felt the bed dip under his weight, the physical closeness only adding to the emotional distance between them. Her heart thudded in her chest as she prepared for whatever was coming next.

"I know you're upset," he began, his voice steady but laced with something Jess couldn't quite place. Was it guilt? "And you have every right to be. I should have been honest with you from the start."

At that, Jess finally looked up, her eyes meeting his. "Honest?" she repeated, the word bitter on her tongue. "Dad, what could you possibly say that would make this better?"

Her father swallowed hard, rubbing his hands together nervously before speaking again. "It's about Amanda... and the money."

Jess's stomach dropped. She had known something was off, but the connection between Amanda and her father's behavior was something she hadn't fully grasped until now. "What do you mean?" she asked, her voice barely above a whisper.

He sighed deeply, running a hand through his thinning hair. "Amanda... she approached me months ago. I didn't know what she was up to at the time, but she offered me an investment opportunity—one that seemed too good to be true." He paused, as though the weight of his words was too heavy to continue. "I took the bait, Jess. I trusted her. I thought… I thought it would help us. We've been struggling financially, more than you know."

Jess's mind raced as she tried to piece everything together. "So you're saying you made some deal with Amanda? That's why you've been acting so weird?"

He nodded, shame washing over his face. "I didn't realize until recently that she was using me. That the whole investment was just part of her plan to get closer to you, to manipulate your reputation." His voice cracked as he added, "I thought I was protecting us, but instead, I put us right in her crosshairs."

Jess stared at him, her emotions warring within her. She wanted to scream, to rage against the unfairness of it all. How could her father have been so naive? How could he have let Amanda worm her way into their lives like this?

"You betrayed me," she finally said, her voice trembling. "Both of you. You and Mom… you knew what she was doing, and you didn't stop it."

Her father's face crumpled, and for the first time, Jess saw the toll this had taken on him. He looked older, more worn, as though the weight of his choices had hollowed him out. "I'm so sorry, Jess," he whispered. "I never wanted this. I never wanted to hurt you."

Jess shook her head, standing up abruptly and moving away from him. She couldn't bear to be near him right now, not when everything felt so raw. "I don't even know who to trust anymore," she said, her voice breaking. "You were supposed to protect me, Dad. You were supposed to have my back, but instead, you've been working with the person who's trying to ruin me."

Her father stood as well, his arms hanging uselessly at his sides. "I know I messed up, Jess. But you have to understand—I didn't know what Amanda was capable of. I thought I was doing the right thing, and by the time I realized the truth, it was too late."

Jess wiped a tear from her cheek, refusing to let herself break down completely in front of him. "It's always too late," she muttered. "Everything is always too late."

Her father took a tentative step toward her. "Please, Jess... let's figure this out together. I'll do whatever it takes to fix this. We can go to the police, we can—"

Jess held up a hand, stopping him. "No," she said firmly. "This isn't something you can just fix. Amanda has been playing all of us for months, and now she's destroyed everything. My reputation, my career... even our family." She shook her head, feeling the anger rise up in her again. "I'm going to deal with this myself. I can't trust anyone else."

Her father's face fell, but Jess didn't give him a chance to respond. She grabbed her phone and headed for the door, her mind already racing with what she needed to do next. Amanda had gone too far, and Jess wasn't going to sit idly by while her life was torn apart. If no one else could help her, then she would handle it herself.

As she walked down the hallway, her mother emerged from the kitchen, her face pale and drawn. "Jess, please," she called softly. "Can we talk?"

Jess's heart clenched at the sight of her mother, but she couldn't stop. Not now. Not when everything was falling apart. "I can't," she said, her voice choked. "I just... I can't."

Without another word, Jess walked out of the house and into the night. The cool air hit her face, but it did little to calm the storm of emotions raging inside her. She pulled out her phone, scrolling through the messages, the posts, the comments. It was all too much. Her mind raced with anger, hurt, and a gnawing sense of betrayal that seemed impossible to shake.

She found herself walking toward the park—the one place she used to go to clear her head when everything became too much. The park had always been a sanctuary for her, a place where she could be herself without the pressures of social media and the constant need to maintain her image. Now, it felt like the only safe space left.

As she sat down on one of the benches, she stared at the sky, the stars flickering faintly above her. She had always loved stargazing, the quiet beauty of the night sky making her feel small in the best way possible. But tonight, even the stars felt distant, as if they, too, were part of the lies she had been living.

Her phone buzzed in her hand, and she glanced down at the screen. Another message, this time from Amanda. The sight of her name made Jess's stomach twist in knots, but she forced herself to open it.

Amanda: "I warned you, Jess. You should have stayed in your lane. Now look where we are."

Jess's hands shook as she read the message. It was another veiled threat, another reminder that Amanda was always one step ahead. But instead of fear, Jess felt a surge of determination. Amanda had taken everything from her—her trust in her friends, her confidence in her family, her reputation—but Jess wasn't going to let her win.

She quickly typed out a response, her fingers moving with a new sense of purpose.

Jess: "This isn't over, Amanda. You think you've won, but you're wrong. I'm not backing down. Not now, not ever."

She hit send, her heart pounding in her chest as she stared at the screen. For the first time in weeks, she felt a spark of hope, a flicker of the fight she had nearly lost.

Amanda may have been playing a dangerous game, but Jess wasn't going to let her walk away unscathed. She had been pushed to her breaking point, but she wasn't broken—not yet. There was still time to turn the tide, to expose Amanda for the manipulative fraud she was.

And Jess Turner, the girl who had built an empire out of likes and lies, was ready for war.

Chapter 8: Breaking Point

The late afternoon sun cast a waning glow over Jess Turner's penthouse apartment, painting the walls in hues of gold and orange. The luxury of her surroundings did little to alleviate the storm brewing inside her. Jess slumped on the plush, white sofa, her once vibrant eyes now shadowed with exhaustion. The endless string of threats, public backlash, and her recent familial betrayals had pushed her to a precipice she hadn't thought possible.

Her phone buzzed on the coffee table, the sound cutting through the oppressive silence. Jess's heart skipped a beat, a reflexive response to the constant state of alert she had been in for weeks. She glanced at the screen, her breath catching as she saw a new message from the anonymous account.

"You think you're safe? You have no idea what's coming. It's time to end this charade."

The message was curt, menacing, and, for the first time, Jess felt a cold shiver down her spine. Her previous sense of determination was now mingled with a profound sense of fear. The threats had escalated from mere accusations to something more sinister, and Jess couldn't ignore the growing sense that this was more than just a campaign of harassment.

With a deep breath, Jess dialed her management team. She needed to hear from them, to find a way out of the maze she was trapped in. The line clicked, and the familiar voice of her manager, Lisa, answered.

"Jess, hey. What's up?" Lisa's voice was upbeat, but Jess could sense an undercurrent of concern.

"I just got another message," Jess said, her voice tight. "It's worse than before."

Lisa was silent for a moment, and Jess could imagine her manager's face shifting from casual to serious. "Alright, let's hear it."

Jess relayed the message, her words punctuated by the clinking of ice cubes in her water glass. When she finished, there was a long pause on the other end.

"Jess, this is getting out of hand," Lisa said finally. "You need to lay low. This situation is volatile."

"I don't want to lay low," Jess snapped, her frustration surfacing. "I want to fight back. But every time I try, it seems like I'm getting pushed further down."

Lisa's voice softened. "I understand. But we need to be strategic. The more you're in the spotlight, the more they can use that against you. You're in a dangerous position."

Jess felt a pang of helplessness. Her entire career was built on being in the spotlight, on being seen and heard. Now, it seemed like the very thing that had made her famous was being used to destroy her.

"I need to do something," Jess said, her voice breaking. "I can't just sit here and wait to be attacked."

Lisa sighed. "Alright. What do you have in mind?"

"I want to confront Amanda," Jess said, her determination rekindled. "She's behind all this. I need to face her directly."

Lisa was silent again, the pause stretching uncomfortably. "Jess, that's a risky move. Amanda is unpredictable, and if she's the one pulling the strings, this could get dangerous."

"I don't care," Jess said, her voice firm. "I need to end this."

"Okay," Lisa finally said. "If you're set on this, we'll support you. But please, be careful. We'll arrange for some security."

Jess hung up, her heart pounding with a mixture of relief and trepidation. The decision had been made. Confronting Amanda was a bold step, but Jess couldn't see another way out. She needed to face her tormentor, to put an end to the lies and threats that had consumed her life.

The next few hours were a whirlwind of activity. Jess and her team made arrangements for a meeting with Amanda. Jess was careful to keep the details of the confrontation under wraps, aware that any leak could undermine her efforts.

As evening approached, Jess found herself standing in front of a chic downtown café, where she had arranged to meet Amanda. The place was a popular spot, known for its sleek decor and upscale clientele. Jess's reflection in the café's glass doors looked unfamiliar to her. Her once-glistening eyes now held a steely resolve, and her confident posture seemed to mask the anxiety that gripped her.

She took a deep breath and stepped inside. The café was buzzing with the soft hum of conversation and the clinking of cutlery. Jess scanned the room, searching for Amanda. It didn't take long for her to spot her rival. Amanda was seated at a corner table, her back straight and her posture exuding an air of haughty indifference.

Jess approached, her steps measured. Amanda looked up as she neared, a smirk curling on her lips. The two women had crossed paths numerous times in the past, but this encounter was charged with a new intensity.

"Jess," Amanda said, her tone dripping with false cheerfulness. "To what do I owe this pleasure?"

"Cut the crap, Amanda," Jess said, her voice low and steady. "We need to talk."

Amanda's eyes narrowed, but she gestured to the empty seat across from her. "Alright, sit down. I'm listening."

Jess took the seat, her heart racing but her demeanor calm. "You've been making my life hell. The threats, the fake evidence—it's all you."

Amanda's smirk widened. "I see you've finally pieced it together. You're quite perceptive when you want to be."

"Why?" Jess asked, her voice cracking slightly despite her effort to remain composed. "Why go through all this trouble to ruin me?"

Amanda leaned back in her chair, her expression a mix of satisfaction and disdain. "You really don't get it, do you? It's not just about you. It's about proving a point. About showing that no one is untouchable."

"You're delusional," Jess said, anger flaring. "You're using me as a pawn in some twisted game."

Amanda's eyes glittered with a dangerous light. "Maybe. Or maybe I'm just tired of watching people like you waltz through life without consequence. You think you're invincible, but you're not."

Jess took a deep breath, trying to steady her shaking hands. "I want this to end. I want you to stop this charade and leave me alone."

Amanda's gaze was unwavering. "And what if I don't?"

Jess's resolve hardened. "Then I'll make sure everyone knows the truth about what you've done. I'll expose you for the fraud you are."

Amanda chuckled, a low, mocking sound. "Do you really think you can? I've made sure every step I've taken is covered. You're in no position to make threats."

The conversation continued, each word a battle in a war that had become deeply personal. Jess's mind raced as she tried to find leverage, a way to turn the tables. The meeting was draining, both emotionally and mentally, and as Jess left the café, she felt the weight of her decision bearing down on her.

The confrontation with Amanda had been as intense as Jess had feared, but it had also made one thing clear: Amanda was not going to back down easily. The stakes were higher than ever, and Jess realized that she was in for a fight that would test every ounce of her strength and resolve.

As she walked back to her penthouse, Jess's thoughts were a maelstrom of fear and determination. The new threatening message had pushed her to a breaking point, but it had also ignited a fire within her. She knew that if she was to reclaim her life and clear her name, she had to confront not just Amanda but also the deeper truths lurking behind the chaos.

The night stretched ahead, filled with unanswered questions and uncertain outcomes. Jess's journey was far from over, and the road ahead promised to be fraught with danger and revelations. But for the first time in a long while, Jess felt a glimmer of hope—a belief that she could still fight back and reclaim her life from the shadows that had haunted her.

Jess paced the floor of her penthouse, her mind racing as she grappled with the decision she had made. The confrontation with Amanda had been as expected—a battle of wills marked by sharp words and bitter accusations. But it had also left Jess with a profound sense of vulnerability. Amanda was a formidable adversary, and Jess knew that confronting her head-on was a risky move that could backfire in ways she hadn't fully anticipated.

The apartment felt eerily quiet after her intense meeting with Amanda. Jess's once-thriving social media empire now seemed like a distant, hollow shell. The glossy images and curated posts that had once defined her were now marred by the chaos that had engulfed her life. Every notification, every comment on her posts, felt like a taunt, a reminder of the mess she was entangled in.

As she tried to compose herself, her phone buzzed again. Jess hesitated before checking it, her heart heavy with dread. The screen displayed a message from an unknown number. She took a deep breath and opened it.

"You think you can confront Amanda and get away with it? You're playing a dangerous game. Watch your back."

The message was chilling, and Jess's pulse quickened. It was clear that the threats were escalating, and the dangers were no longer confined to the digital realm. She needed a plan, a strategy that would allow her to fight back while keeping herself safe.

Jess sat down at her desk and opened her laptop. She needed to gather as much information as possible, to understand the full extent of Amanda's scheme and find any potential weaknesses. The evening stretched ahead, and Jess poured herself into research, her focus unwavering.

Amanda had been clever in her manipulation, using her influence to plant seeds of doubt and create a web of deceit. Jess knew that exposing Amanda's scheme required more than just confronting her; it required evidence that could withstand public scrutiny and legal challenges.

The hours ticked by, and Jess's research revealed some critical pieces of information. Amanda had not acted alone. There were signs that indicated a larger network of influencers and possibly even a shadowy group behind her. Jess's suspicion grew that this was not just a personal vendetta but part of a more extensive operation to manipulate public perception and control narratives.

As Jess worked, her thoughts kept returning to the meeting with Amanda. The smugness in Amanda's demeanor, the way she had taunted Jess—it all pointed to someone who felt secure in their position. Amanda believed she was untouchable, and that confidence made her dangerous.

Jess's phone buzzed again, breaking her concentration. This time, it was a message from Daniel, an old friend who had recently reached out. Daniel had been a confidant in Jess's early days on social media, someone she trusted implicitly. She opened the message, hoping for a glimmer of hope.

"Hey Jess, I've been following what's been happening. I might have some information that could help. Can we talk?"

Jess's heart lifted slightly. Daniel's offer of help was a welcome distraction from the overwhelming darkness of her situation. She quickly replied, arranging to meet him at a quiet café the next morning.

The following day, Jess arrived at the café early, her mind still reeling from the previous night's discoveries. The café was a small, unassuming place with a cozy atmosphere—perfect for a confidential conversation. Daniel was already there, sitting at a corner table. He looked up as Jess approached, his face reflecting a mixture of concern and determination.

"Jess," he said, standing up to greet her. "I'm really sorry to hear about everything you're going through."

"Thanks, Daniel," Jess replied, taking a seat. "I appreciate you reaching out. What do you have for me?"

Daniel pulled out his laptop and began to show Jess some documents and emails he had gathered. "I've been digging around, trying to piece together what's been going on. I found some connections between Amanda and several other influencers who have a history of engaging in manipulative practices."

Jess leaned forward, her interest piqued. "What kind of connections?"

"From what I've found," Daniel explained, "Amanda isn't working alone. She's part of a network that's been involved in several high-profile scandals. They manipulate public opinion, create fake controversies, and use their influence to control the narrative."

Jess's mind raced as she absorbed the information. This was bigger than she had imagined. "So, Amanda's just a pawn in a larger game?"

"Exactly," Daniel said. "And it gets worse. There's evidence that this network has been targeting other influencers and celebrities as well, using similar tactics to discredit them and boost their own profiles."

Jess felt a surge of both fear and determination. If this network was behind the threats and lies, it meant that Amanda was only a part of the problem. The scale of the operation was far more extensive than she had initially thought.

"We need to expose this," Jess said firmly. "But we have to be careful. If this network is as powerful as it seems, they won't take kindly to being exposed."

Daniel nodded. "I agree. I've been working on a plan to gather more evidence and find a way to leak it safely. But it's going to require careful coordination and a lot of secrecy."

Jess's resolve hardened. The confrontation with Amanda had been a critical step, but now she had to think strategically. "What do you need from me?"

"First," Daniel said, "we need to solidify the evidence we have and identify key players in the network. Then, we need to figure out the best way to release the information without putting ourselves at risk."

The conversation turned into a detailed discussion of their next steps. Jess and Daniel planned to gather more evidence, reach out to trusted contacts, and prepare for a public reveal. Jess's mind buzzed with the possibilities and challenges ahead. She knew that this was just the beginning of a complex and dangerous battle.

As they wrapped up their meeting, Jess felt a renewed sense of purpose. For the first time in weeks, she had a concrete plan and a partner she could trust. The road ahead was fraught with danger, but Jess was determined to see it through.

Back at her penthouse, Jess reviewed her notes and prepared for the next phase of their plan. The pressure was immense, and the stakes were high, but she was ready to fight back against the lies and deceit that had threatened to destroy her life.

As night fell, Jess stared out at the city lights, reflecting on how far she had come. The fight was far from over, but she was no longer alone. With Daniel's help, she had a chance to expose the truth and reclaim her life. The journey ahead would be perilous, but Jess was ready to face whatever came next.

Chapter 9: The Unexpected Ally

Jess had barely managed a few hours of restless sleep after her intense confrontation with Amanda. The shadows of doubt and worry had crept into her dreams, blending with the harsh reality of her waking hours. The threats, the lies, and the relentless scrutiny from the public had created a storm of anxiety that seemed impossible to navigate. Yet amidst the chaos, a glimmer of hope emerged in the form of Daniel, an old friend who had resurfaced with potentially crucial information.

The following morning, Jess found herself at a small café downtown, a quiet refuge from the prying eyes of the city and the oppressive weight of her current situation. The sun filtered through the large windows, casting a warm glow over the space, but Jess felt anything but warm. Her mind was consumed with the details of her meeting with Daniel and the possible impact of the information he had promised.

Daniel arrived punctually, carrying a messenger bag that seemed to contain more than just the usual essentials. His demeanor was calm, but there was an underlying urgency in his eyes. Jess noticed the tension in his posture as he approached, and she felt a surge of gratitude for his willingness to help.

"Hey, Jess," Daniel greeted, his voice steady. "I'm glad you could meet."

"Thanks for coming through, Daniel," Jess replied. "What have you got for me?"

They settled into a quiet corner of the café, away from the hustle and bustle. Daniel placed his bag on the table and began to pull out a series of documents and printouts. Jess leaned forward, her heart racing with anticipation.

"Over the past few days," Daniel began, "I've been digging into Amanda's background and connections. What I've found might be the key to turning this whole situation around."

Jess nodded, her focus solely on the documents Daniel was laying out. "Go ahead. I'm all ears."

Daniel flipped open a folder, revealing a collection of printed emails, screenshots, and notes. "Amanda has been working with a network of influencers who specialize in creating scandals and manipulating public opinion. This network is extensive and operates in secrecy, but their influence is significant."

Jess studied the documents closely. "So, Amanda isn't acting alone. Who else is involved?"

"That's the tricky part," Daniel said. "From what I've gathered, there are several key players, but they're all very cautious about revealing their identities. They use pseudonyms and fake accounts to avoid detection. However, I've managed to trace some of their activities back to a central figure—a person who seems to be orchestrating much of this chaos."

Jess's mind raced. "Do you have any leads on this central figure?"

"Not directly," Daniel admitted. "But I've identified some recurring patterns and connections that might lead us to them.

The central figure seems to be the mastermind behind many of these manipulations, including the threats against you."

Jess felt a mix of frustration and determination. "We need to find this person and expose them. Amanda's scheme is bad enough, but if there's someone else pulling the strings, we need to know who they are."

Daniel agreed. "Exactly. I've also found evidence suggesting that this network has been involved in similar schemes against other influencers. It's a pattern of harassment and deceit that they've been using to advance their own agendas."

As Jess reviewed the documents, she began to see the extent of Amanda's manipulative tactics. The emails detailed plans to fabricate evidence, create fake accounts, and spread false narratives. The sophistication of the scheme was staggering, and Jess felt a renewed sense of urgency to bring it to light.

"We need to be strategic about this," Jess said. "If we just release everything at once, it might get lost in the noise or be dismissed as another attack on Amanda."

"Agreed," Daniel said. "We need to build a strong case with concrete evidence and find a way to present it that will resonate with the public and the media. It's also crucial that we protect ourselves from any potential retaliation."

Jess felt a wave of anxiety at the thought of retaliation. The threats she had received were already unnerving enough, and the prospect of facing a powerful network of manipulators was daunting. Yet she knew that taking action was the only way to regain control of her life and clear her name.

"What's our first step?" Jess asked, her voice steady despite her apprehension.

"First, we need to gather more evidence," Daniel explained. "We should focus on tracing the connections between Amanda and the central figure, and also identify any other influencers who might be involved. Once we have a comprehensive picture, we can start planning our next move."

Jess nodded, feeling a sense of resolve. "Let's do it. I want to get to the bottom of this and put an end to it."

Daniel and Jess spent the next few hours working together, poring over documents and analyzing connections. The café's cozy atmosphere provided a stark contrast to the gravity of their task, but the work was crucial. As they dug deeper, they uncovered more details about the network's operations and their tactics.

Daniel's laptop revealed several encrypted messages and hidden accounts that hinted at the network's internal communications. Jess was impressed by Daniel's diligence and resourcefulness. His expertise was a valuable asset, and she felt a growing sense of trust in his ability to help her navigate this treacherous situation.

As the day wore on, Jess and Daniel made significant progress in their investigation. They identified several key players in the network and uncovered patterns that linked them to Amanda's scheme. Jess felt a surge of hope as the pieces of the puzzle began to come together.

"Okay," Jess said, closing her laptop with a sense of accomplishment. "We've made good progress today. What's next?"

Daniel looked thoughtful. "Next, we need to secure our findings and prepare for the next phase. We should consider reaching out to trusted media contacts who can help us get the story out in a way that's impactful and credible."

Jess agreed. "I'll start reaching out to my media contacts and see if we can find a way to leverage their platforms. It's crucial that we get the truth out there."

As Jess and Daniel wrapped up their meeting, Jess felt a renewed sense of purpose. The road ahead was still fraught with challenges, but with Daniel's help, she felt better equipped to face them. The fight was far from over, but for the first time in a long while, Jess felt a glimmer of hope that justice might be within reach.

As they parted ways, Jess couldn't shake the feeling that the battle was just beginning. The network's power and influence were formidable, and the stakes were high. Yet Jess was determined to see it through, to expose the truth and reclaim her life from the grip of deceit and manipulation.

The next few days would be critical in shaping the outcome of her fight. With Daniel's assistance and the evidence they had gathered, Jess knew she had a fighting chance. The challenge now was to navigate the complex web of deception and bring the truth to light, no matter the cost.

Jess was determined to execute her plan with precision, but the reality of her situation quickly started to overshadow her optimism. The days following her meeting with Daniel were marked by mounting obstacles and increasing desperation. Amanda's ability to anticipate and counter their moves was beginning to take its toll on Jess's resolve.

The first sign of trouble came within hours of their plan taking shape. Jess had carefully coordinated with Daniel to release a small portion of their findings to trusted media contacts. They hoped to gain a foothold in the narrative and start shifting public opinion. However, before they could even make their first move, Amanda's counter-offensive began.

Jess woke up to a flurry of notifications. Her phone buzzed incessantly as she scrolled through the messages. The latest post on Amanda's account was a well-crafted piece of propaganda designed to undermine Jess's credibility further. Amanda had managed to spin the narrative to suggest that Jess and Daniel were simply creating a diversion from their own alleged criminal activities. The post was accompanied by fabricated screenshots and misleading captions, all aimed at discrediting Jess's efforts.

Jess's heart sank as she read the comments flooding in, many of which were filled with vitriol and accusations. The public's perception was already shifting against her once again. The comments ranged from accusations of deception to demands for her to step away from the limelight. The cycle of attack and counter-attack seemed endless, and Jess felt trapped in a never-ending spiral of public scorn and media manipulation.

Determined not to let Amanda's tactics derail their progress, Jess contacted Daniel. They met at a different café, one more secluded and secure than their previous meeting spot. Jess arrived early, hoping to gather her thoughts and prepare for what was to come.

Daniel arrived soon after, carrying a fresh batch of documents. His face was lined with worry, reflecting the mounting pressure they both felt. He placed the documents on the table and took a deep breath before speaking.

"We've hit a snag," Daniel said, his voice heavy with frustration. "Amanda's counterattacks are more coordinated than we anticipated. She's using our own evidence against us and turning public sentiment even more against you."

Jess nodded, her mind racing through possible solutions. "We need to find a way to turn this around. We can't let her control the narrative any longer."

"I've been thinking," Daniel said, "that we need to go on the offensive, but with a different approach. We need to expose the full extent of Amanda's manipulation and tie it to the network behind her. If we can present undeniable proof of their involvement, we might be able to regain some control."

Jess agreed, feeling a renewed sense of determination. "Okay, let's focus on gathering that proof and preparing a comprehensive report. We need to make sure it's airtight."

For the next few days, Jess and Daniel worked tirelessly. They delved deeper into Amanda's connections and scrutinized the network's activities. They cross-referenced their findings with public records and interviewed sources who might have insight into Amanda's schemes. The effort was exhaustive and draining, but Jess remained resolute.

As they pieced together the puzzle, Jess began to uncover more about Amanda's collaborators and their tactics. The network wasn't just a group of influencers; it was a sophisticated operation with various subgroups dedicated to different aspects of manipulation and deceit. The more Jess learned, the clearer it became that exposing this network would be a monumental task.

One night, while reviewing the latest batch of evidence, Jess received a call from Daniel. His voice was urgent and edged with concern.

"Jess, you need to see this," Daniel said. "I've just come across something that could be a game-changer."

Jess's pulse quickened. "What is it?"

"I've located a hidden forum where Amanda and her network discuss their operations. There's a thread where they talk about their plans to discredit you and manipulate the media. The level of detail and coordination is shocking."

Jess's heart raced as she listened. "Can you get me access to that forum?"

"I'm working on it," Daniel said. "But it's heavily encrypted, and I'm still trying to crack it. In the meantime, I think we should prepare a press release that outlines what we've discovered so far. We need to be ready to act as soon as we have solid proof."

Jess agreed, and they spent the next few hours drafting a press release that would highlight the manipulation and deceit they had uncovered. The document was carefully worded to present their findings without giving Amanda and her network any opportunity to counterattack.

As the days passed, Jess and Daniel faced increasing pressure. The media continued to amplify Amanda's accusations, and Jess's public image suffered further damage. Despite their best efforts, it felt as though they were constantly on the defensive.

Then, just when Jess thought things couldn't get any worse, she received another anonymous message. The message contained a threat that was more personal and menacing than any she had received before. It detailed plans to ruin not just her career but her personal life as well. The threat was a chilling reminder of the stakes involved and the lengths to which Amanda and her network were willing to go.

Feeling overwhelmed but not defeated, Jess and Daniel pressed on. They managed to gain access to the hidden forum, and the information they found was damning. The forum contained detailed plans and communications that confirmed the extent of Amanda's manipulation and the involvement of other key players in the network.

With this new evidence in hand, Jess felt a renewed sense of purpose. She and Daniel worked around the clock to prepare a comprehensive exposé that would reveal the full extent of Amanda's scheme and the network behind her. They aimed to make the evidence undeniable and compelling, hoping to shift the tide in their favor.

Finally, the day arrived when Jess and Daniel were ready to release their findings. They held a press conference where Jess presented the evidence, detailing the manipulations, threats, and deceit that had been orchestrated against her. The exposé was thorough and well-documented, leaving no room for doubt.

The press conference was a turning point. The evidence presented was so compelling that it forced many media outlets to reconsider their stance on the issue. The public reaction was swift and intense, with many people expressing outrage at the extent of Amanda's manipulations.

Jess felt a surge of relief as she saw the tide beginning to turn. The public's perception of her began to shift, and the scrutiny that had once been focused on her was now directed at Amanda and her network. The fight was far from over, but for the first time in weeks, Jess felt as though she had regained some control over the situation.

Despite the progress, Jess knew that the battle was not yet won. Amanda and her network were still a threat, and the road to fully clearing her name was long and uncertain. But with Daniel's help and the evidence they had gathered, Jess felt more equipped to face the challenges ahead.

As Jess and Daniel wrapped up their press conference, Jess took a moment to reflect on the journey so far. The experience had tested her in ways she had never imagined, but it had also revealed the strength and resilience she didn't know she had. The fight was far from over, but Jess was ready to face whatever came next, armed with the truth and the support of those who truly cared for her.

Chapter 10: Revelation

Jess sat at her desk in her dimly lit apartment, surrounded by a chaotic mess of papers, files, and electronic devices. The weight of the ongoing battle against Amanda and her network seemed to press heavily on her shoulders. Her eyes were tired, and her mind was consumed with the ceaseless effort to piece together the complex puzzle that had shattered her life. Despite the sleepless nights and mounting frustration, she remained resolute in her pursuit of justice.

Daniel had been a crucial ally throughout this ordeal, but as they delved deeper into Amanda's schemes, the situation grew increasingly complicated. They had uncovered significant evidence pointing to Amanda's manipulative tactics, but the deeper they dug, the more they realized that Amanda was not working alone. The web of deceit extended far beyond what they had initially suspected.

It was late afternoon when Jess received the breakthrough she had been desperately hoping for. Daniel had sent her an urgent message, suggesting that he had discovered a crucial piece of evidence. Jess's heart raced as she opened the encrypted file Daniel had shared. The file contained a series of communications from a hidden forum that Amanda's network had used to plan their attacks.

The documents revealed something Jess hadn't anticipated: Amanda's manipulations were part of a much larger and more organized operation involving several high-profile influencers. The network's goal wasn't just to discredit Jess but to control and influence public perception on a grand scale. The documents outlined a series of tactics, including fabricating evidence, staging false controversies, and leveraging their influence to sway public opinion.

Jess's hands shook as she read through the documents. The level of sophistication in the operation was staggering. It became clear that Amanda's actions were part of a broader strategy to manipulate online narratives and maintain control over the digital space. The documents also hinted at connections between Amanda and several other influential figures, each with their own motives and agendas.

The most shocking revelation came from an internal communication within the network. It detailed a planned "final act" that involved staging a dramatic event to solidify their control and discredit anyone who posed a threat to their dominance. Jess realized that this "final act" was likely a culmination of Amanda's scheme to ruin her reputation once and for all.

Jess felt a mix of anger and determination as she absorbed the gravity of the situation. This wasn't just about clearing her name anymore; it was about exposing a corrupt system that sought to manipulate and control public perception. The stakes had escalated dramatically, and Jess knew that they had to act swiftly and decisively.

She immediately called Daniel to discuss their next steps. As she waited for him to pick up, her mind raced with potential strategies. The revelations needed to be carefully handled to avoid giving Amanda's network an opportunity to counter their moves. Jess's heart pounded as she prepared to face the challenges ahead.

When Daniel answered the call, his voice was tense but determined. "Jess, I'm glad you saw the documents. This changes everything."

"I know," Jess replied, her voice steady despite her nerves. "Amanda's network is much more extensive than we thought. We need to expose this on a larger scale."

Daniel agreed. "We have to go beyond just clearing your name. We need to reveal the entire network and their tactics. If we do this right, we can not only discredit Amanda but also shed light on how this manipulation affects the public."

Jess and Daniel began to plan their strategy for revealing the truth. They needed to craft a comprehensive exposé that would not only highlight Amanda's schemes but also expose the network's broader agenda. Their goal was to provide undeniable evidence that would force the media and the public to confront the reality of the situation.

The task was daunting. Jess and Daniel worked tirelessly, compiling evidence, drafting reports, and preparing a detailed presentation. They knew that their findings would face intense scrutiny and potential backlash, but they were committed to seeing the truth exposed.

As they prepared their materials, Jess couldn't help but reflect on the personal toll this journey had taken on her. The public scrutiny, the betrayal of those she once trusted, and the constant fear of further attacks had left her emotionally and physically drained. But she also felt a renewed sense of purpose and determination. This fight had become about more than just her reputation; it was about holding those who sought to manipulate and deceive accountable.

One evening, as Jess reviewed the final draft of their exposé, she received a phone call from an unexpected source. It was her mother, who had been distant and preoccupied throughout the ordeal. Jess was taken aback by the call and hesitated before answering.

"Jess, I've been following everything that's been happening," her mother's voice was strained. "I know I haven't been there for you, but I want to help. I have information that might be crucial to your case."

Jess's heart skipped a beat. "What kind of information?"

"There are things I've kept from you," her mother said, her voice trembling. "Secrets about Amanda and her network. I didn't want to involve you, but now I realize that I was wrong. I need to come clean and help you expose the truth."

Jess felt a surge of hope mixed with apprehension. "I appreciate your offer, but you need to tell me everything you know. We can't afford any more surprises."

Her mother agreed to meet Jess in person. The meeting was set for the following day, and Jess felt a mix of anticipation and anxiety. She hoped that the information her mother had could provide the final pieces needed to fully unravel Amanda's scheme.

As Jess prepared for the meeting, she couldn't help but think about how her relationship with her mother had been strained throughout this ordeal. The distance between them had added to the burden of the situation. She hoped that this meeting would not only provide crucial information but also begin to mend the fractured relationship.

The next day, Jess met her mother at a quiet café, away from the public eye. The café's tranquil atmosphere contrasted sharply with the chaos of Jess's current life. Jess's mother arrived, looking weary but determined. They exchanged a tense greeting before Jess led her to a secluded table.

"I'm sorry for how things have been," Jess's mother began, her voice soft. "I've been scared and confused, and I didn't know how to help."

Jess nodded, her expression guarded. "I appreciate you coming forward. What do you have to tell me?"

Her mother took a deep breath and began to recount her knowledge. She revealed that Amanda's network had been involved in a series of covert operations to manipulate public opinion and silence dissent. Her mother had been indirectly involved in some of these operations through her work with various online marketing firms. Although she wasn't directly responsible for the manipulations, she had unwittingly been a part of the system.

Jess listened intently as her mother explained how Amanda and her network had used a combination of psychological tactics and financial incentives to influence key players in the industry. The network had leveraged their connections to plant false narratives and control the flow of information. Jess's mother also revealed that she had witnessed some of the network's inner workings and had seen how Amanda used her influence to target individuals who posed a threat to her agenda.

The information was invaluable. Jess could see how the pieces of the puzzle were coming together. Her mother's revelations provided crucial insights into the network's tactics and confirmed many of the suspicions Jess had held. The final piece of the puzzle was now in place.

As Jess absorbed the information, she felt a mix of relief and frustration. The road to uncovering the truth had been long and arduous, and the emotional toll had been significant. But with her mother's help and the evidence they had gathered, Jess felt a renewed sense of purpose.

The next steps were clear. Jess and Daniel would finalize their exposé and prepare to release it to the public. They needed to ensure that their findings were presented in a way that would withstand scrutiny and make a compelling case against Amanda and her network.

As Jess left the café, she felt a flicker of hope. The journey had been fraught with challenges and setbacks, but the revelations had given her a renewed sense of determination. She was ready to face the final stage of the battle and expose the truth, no matter the cost.

Jess's mind raced as she processed the revelation that Amanda's scheme was not a solitary effort but part of a much larger conspiracy. The realization that there was a second, hidden agenda behind the anonymous messages sent a jolt of anxiety through her. This new twist meant that Amanda was not the sole architect of Jess's downfall, and the stakes were even higher than before.

Determined to uncover the full extent of the conspiracy, Jess knew she had to act quickly. She and Daniel worked late into the night, finalizing their exposé with the new evidence they had gathered. Their goal was to expose the entire network and the hidden figure behind the second set of anonymous messages.

The following morning, Jess and Daniel met at a secluded location to review their plan. Jess was anxious but resolute. The pressure of revealing the truth weighed heavily on her, but she was committed to seeing it through. The plan was to release a detailed report to the media, accompanied by undeniable evidence that would expose Amanda's manipulation and the involvement of the second conspirator.

As they finalized their strategy, Jess received another message from the anonymous account. This one was different—more insidious. It threatened not only her reputation but also suggested that her safety was at risk. The message implied that there were more dangerous consequences awaiting her if she proceeded with her plan.

Jess felt a shiver run down her spine. The threats had become more personal and menacing, reflecting the growing desperation of those trying to keep their secrets buried. Despite her fear, Jess knew that backing down was not an option. She had come too far and uncovered too much to let the conspirators win.

With the final details in place, Jess and Daniel prepared to go public. They coordinated with a trusted journalist who had previously covered the initial controversy surrounding Jess. The journalist, Emily Carter, had proven to be fair and thorough, and Jess felt she could trust her to handle the story with the integrity it deserved.

The release was scheduled for the next day, and Jess felt a mix of anticipation and dread. She knew that exposing the truth would be a double-edged sword—it would reveal the full extent of the manipulation but also subject her to even more public scrutiny and backlash.

As Jess and Daniel went over the final draft of their exposé, Jess's phone rang. It was her mother, calling to check in. The conversation was strained, and Jess could sense her mother's apprehension.

"Jess, are you sure about this?" her mother's voice wavered. "This could put you in even more danger."

Jess took a deep breath. "I have to do this, Mom. The truth needs to come out. It's the only way to stop this nightmare."

Her mother sighed, resigned but supportive. "I understand. Just be careful. I'll be here if you need anything."

With the final preparations complete, Jess and Daniel met with Emily Carter to hand over the evidence and discuss the release. Emily listened intently, asking probing questions and ensuring that every detail was accurately represented. Jess and Daniel provided her with a comprehensive overview of the network's manipulative tactics and the newly discovered evidence of the second conspirator's involvement.

As the day of the release approached, Jess couldn't shake the feeling of impending doom. The threats from the anonymous account and the mounting pressure of going public had taken a toll on her. She tried to focus on the importance of their mission and the potential impact of exposing the truth.

Finally, the day arrived. The exposé was published, and the media frenzy erupted almost immediately. The detailed report outlined Amanda's elaborate scheme to tarnish Jess's reputation, complete with fabricated evidence and staged controversies. It also revealed the involvement of the second conspirator, a prominent social media influencer who had secretly collaborated with Amanda to manipulate public perception.

The response from the public and the media was swift and intense. Reactions ranged from shock and outrage to disbelief and support for Jess. The story dominated headlines, and the online discourse was ablaze with discussions about the revelations. Many of Jess's followers expressed their support, while others criticized her for not uncovering the truth sooner.

In the midst of the media storm, Jess felt a mix of vindication and trepidation. The exposure of Amanda and the second conspirator's tactics was a significant victory, but it also meant that Jess was now at the center of a larger controversy. She was inundated with messages from the media, requests for interviews, and reactions from her followers.

Despite the chaos, Jess remained focused on her next steps. She knew that exposing Amanda and the second conspirator was only part of the battle. The aftermath of the revelations would be crucial in determining how she would move forward and rebuild her life.

As Jess and Daniel continued to navigate the fallout from the exposé, they received an unexpected visit from Emily Carter. Emily had new information that added another layer to the unfolding drama. She had uncovered evidence suggesting that the second conspirator was not acting alone and that there were other influential figures involved in the conspiracy.

Emily's findings revealed a network of influencers who had been using their platforms to manipulate public opinion and control narratives. The evidence pointed to a coordinated effort to undermine anyone who threatened their dominance. This new revelation was a game-changer and added another dimension to the ongoing saga.

Jess felt a renewed sense of determination as she absorbed the new information. The fight to expose the truth had become even more complex, but she was committed to seeing it through. She knew that the road ahead would be challenging, but she was ready to face whatever came next.

As the days went by, Jess and Daniel continued to work with Emily to unravel the full extent of the conspiracy. They coordinated with law enforcement and legal experts to ensure that the evidence was properly handled and that those responsible would be held accountable.

Throughout this process, Jess reflected on the personal toll the ordeal had taken on her. The betrayal, public scrutiny, and emotional strain had been immense, but she had also learned valuable lessons about trust, integrity, and resilience. She was determined to use her experience to advocate for greater transparency and accountability in the digital age.

Chapter 11: The Truth Unveiled

The morning after the exposé broke, Jess awoke to a frenzy of notifications. Her phone buzzed incessantly as news outlets, followers, and even strangers weighed in on the scandal. The fallout from the revelations about Amanda and the newly discovered conspirator had sent shockwaves through the digital world. The intricate web of lies, manipulations, and deceit was now laid bare for everyone to see.

Jess sat on the edge of her bed, staring at the barrage of headlines that flashed across her screen. The once-familiar comfort of her luxurious life felt alien and distant. The glossy veneer of fame had shattered, leaving her exposed and vulnerable. Jess's mind raced as she tried to process the enormity of what had transpired.

The exposé had not only revealed Amanda's scheme but also uncovered the identity of the additional conspirator—an influential figure in the social media landscape who had secretly collaborated with Amanda. The full extent of their manipulations had been detailed, including how they had orchestrated various smear campaigns against Jess, created fake evidence, and exploited their followers to sow discord and mistrust.

Jess had arranged a meeting with her management team and Daniel to discuss their next steps. She needed to navigate the aftermath carefully and determine how to address the myriad of issues that had arisen. The impact of the revelations was immense, and Jess understood that managing public perception and mitigating further damage was crucial.

As she arrived at the conference room, Jess was greeted by her team, who looked equally stressed and concerned. The room was filled with a tense energy as they settled into their seats, preparing to tackle the fallout.

"Jess, we need to address the situation immediately," her manager, Laura, began. "The media is in overdrive, and the backlash is intense. We need a strategy to manage the public relations aspect and to clarify our position."

Jess nodded, trying to steady her nerves. "I understand. We need to be transparent about what happened and ensure that everyone knows the truth. But we also need to consider how this will affect my brand and personal life."

Daniel, who had been a steadfast ally throughout the ordeal, spoke up. "Jess, the most important thing now is to stay focused on the truth. The public needs to understand the full scope of the conspiracy and how Amanda and the conspirator manipulated the situation."

Laura nodded in agreement. "We've already begun drafting a comprehensive statement to address the revelations. It will include details of how the manipulations were carried out and the steps we're taking to hold those responsible accountable."

Jess took a deep breath, feeling the weight of the moment. "Let's move forward with the statement, but we also need to think about the longer-term implications. I want to ensure that we're not just addressing the immediate fallout but also working on rebuilding trust and credibility."

The team began discussing the details of the statement, outlining how they would present the evidence and address the public's concerns. The goal was to provide a clear and honest account of what had transpired while also highlighting Jess's commitment to integrity and transparency.

As the meeting progressed, Jess's thoughts kept drifting back to her personal relationships. The revelations had strained her connections with her family and friends, and she was grappling with feelings of betrayal and isolation. Her father's financial motives and her mother's reluctance to act had left her reeling. The trust that once bound them together had been shattered, and Jess felt the weight of their actions pressing heavily on her.

Determined to address the personal aspects of the fallout, Jess decided to reach out to her family. She wanted to have an open and honest conversation about the impact of the revelations and to seek a path toward reconciliation. Jess knew that rebuilding her life would require mending these fractured relationships.

She arranged a family meeting, hoping to clear the air and address the lingering issues. The meeting took place at her parents' home, a place that once represented comfort and security but now felt charged with tension.

As Jess arrived, her mother greeted her with a tight hug. Her father stood by the doorway, looking uneasy. The room was filled with an air of apprehension as Jess sat down at the dining table, ready to confront the difficult conversation ahead.

"I wanted to talk to you both about everything that's happened," Jess began, trying to keep her voice steady. "I know things have been strained, and I need to understand where we go from here."

Her mother, tears welling in her eyes, spoke first. "Jess, we're so sorry for not being more supportive. We were scared and didn't know how to handle everything. I should have been more honest with you about what I knew."

Jess nodded, her heart aching at her mother's admission. "I understand that you were trying to protect me, but the lack of transparency made things worse. I felt abandoned and betrayed."

Her father, who had been quiet until now, took a deep breath. "Jess, I made mistakes. I let my financial troubles cloud my judgment, and I didn't handle things the way I should have. I'm sorry for how my actions contributed to the mess."

The conversation was emotional and raw, with Jess expressing her hurt and frustration while her parents offered apologies and explanations. It was clear that rebuilding trust would be a long process, but Jess felt a glimmer of hope that they could start to mend their relationship.

After the family meeting, Jess felt emotionally drained but somewhat relieved. The conversations had been difficult, but they had opened the door to healing. Jess knew that the road to rebuilding her life would be challenging, but she was determined to move forward with clarity and purpose.

The fallout from the revelations continued to unfold, with the media coverage evolving as new details emerged. Jess remained in the public eye, handling interviews and statements with the help of her management team. The process of confronting Amanda and the conspirator had taken its toll, but Jess was committed to seeing it through and ensuring that those responsible faced justice.

In the days that followed, Jess and Daniel continued to work with legal experts to pursue further actions against Amanda and the conspirator. They gathered additional evidence and built a case to hold them accountable for their actions. The legal process was complex and time-consuming, but Jess remained resolute in her pursuit of justice.

The aftermath of the revelations hit Jess with an unexpected intensity. The initial shock of exposing Amanda and the additional conspirator had barely begun to settle when the true scale of the fallout became apparent. Jess found herself at the center of a media storm, with the truth about the manipulations spreading rapidly across news outlets, social media, and every conceivable platform.

In the days following the exposé, Jess's life was a whirlwind of interviews, apologies, and damage control. The public's reaction was a mix of disbelief, sympathy, and condemnation. While some applauded her bravery for exposing the truth, others criticized her for her role in the scandal and questioned her judgment. The barrage of opinions, both positive and negative, was overwhelming.

Jess's management team worked tirelessly to manage the crisis. Laura, her manager, was in constant communication with the media, issuing statements and attempting to steer the narrative in a more favorable direction. Daniel, her ally and former friend, played a crucial role in supporting Jess through the tumultuous period, providing both practical assistance and emotional support.

Despite their best efforts, Jess struggled to find a sense of normalcy. Her phone was inundated with messages from journalists, fans, and even former acquaintances, each seeking a piece of her story. Social media, once a source of validation and connection, had become a battleground where her every move was scrutinized and dissected.

In a rare moment of solitude, Jess sat alone in her apartment, surrounded by the quiet chaos of her disrupted life. The once-vibrant space now felt cold and distant. She stared at the reflection of her own image in a nearby mirror, seeing not the confident, glamorous persona her followers were accustomed to but a young woman grappling with profound betrayal and disillusionment.

The revelations had not only affected her public image but had also strained her personal relationships. Her interactions with her family had become strained, with unresolved issues lingering like shadows in their conversations. The betrayal of her closest friend, Rachel, and the revelations about her family's involvement had left Jess feeling isolated and disconnected.

Determined to address the personal fallout, Jess reached out to her family again. She arranged a meeting with her parents, hoping to have a candid conversation about their future together and how they could rebuild their strained relationship.

The meeting took place in a small, neutral setting—one that felt less charged with the intensity of their previous encounters. Jess's parents arrived with an air of reluctance, their faces reflecting the weight of their own guilt and regret.

"Thank you for coming," Jess began, trying to keep her tone calm. "I think it's important that we talk openly about what's happened and how we move forward."

Her mother, who had been more reserved during their previous meetings, spoke first. "Jess, we've been thinking a lot about everything that's happened. We realize now how much we've let you down, and we want to make things right."

Jess nodded, her heart heavy with mixed emotions. "I appreciate that, but it's going to take time for me to process everything. I need to understand why things happened the way they did and how we can rebuild our trust."

Her father, who had been quiet until now, took a deep breath. "Jess, I know I made mistakes. My financial troubles led me to make poor decisions, and I didn't handle things the way I should have. I'm deeply sorry for the impact it's had on you."

The conversation was difficult but necessary. Jess's parents expressed their remorse and outlined their plans to make amends. They agreed to work on rebuilding their relationship with Jess and to seek professional counseling to address the underlying issues that had contributed to the betrayal.

While the conversation provided some measure of relief, Jess knew that rebuilding trust would be a long and arduous process. She was determined to work through the issues with her family, but she also recognized the need to focus on her own healing and recovery.

As Jess continued to navigate the fallout from the revelations, she took a step back from her social media presence. The decision to temporarily disconnect from the digital world was a conscious effort to regain her sense of self and to find clarity amidst the chaos. Jess's absence from social media was both a relief and a challenge. It provided her with the space to reflect on her experiences and to focus on personal growth, but it also left her feeling disconnected from the world she had once been so deeply immersed in.

During this period of introspection, Jess sought solace in her personal relationships and in activities that had once brought her joy. She reconnected with old friends, pursued hobbies she had neglected, and engaged in self-care practices to help her heal from the emotional wounds inflicted by the scandal.

One of the most significant aspects of Jess's journey was her ongoing commitment to uncovering the full extent of the conspiracy. Despite the personal toll, she remained dedicated to ensuring that Amanda and the additional conspirator faced justice for their actions. Jess worked closely with her legal team to pursue further actions and to hold those responsible accountable.

The legal process was complex and often frustrating, with numerous obstacles and delays. However, Jess remained resolute, knowing that pursuing justice was an essential part of her healing journey. The pursuit of accountability also served as a way to reclaim her narrative and to demonstrate her commitment to truth and integrity.

As Jess's personal and legal battles continued, she also began to reflect on the broader implications of her experiences. The revelations had exposed the darker side of the social media landscape—the manipulation, deceit, and exploitation that often lurked beneath the surface. Jess's journey through deception and betrayal had provided her with valuable insights into the impact of social media on personal relationships, self-worth, and authenticity.

In a series of interviews and public statements, Jess spoke candidly about her experiences, emphasizing the importance of honesty and transparency. She used her platform to advocate for positive change within the social media industry and to raise awareness about the dangers of online manipulation and deceit.

The public response to Jess's advocacy was mixed. While some praised her efforts to address the issues within the social media landscape, others criticized her for bringing attention to the problems without offering concrete solutions. Jess remained focused on her mission, understanding that change was a gradual process and that her efforts were just one part of a larger conversation.

As Jess worked to rebuild her life and reputation, she found strength in her personal growth and resilience. The challenges she had faced had tested her character and revealed her inner strength. Jess emerged from the experience with a renewed sense of purpose and a commitment to living authentically.

The chapter concluded with Jess standing at a crossroads, having faced the fallout from the revelations and the personal impact of the scandal. She reflected on her journey through deception, betrayal, and public scrutiny, recognizing the lessons she had learned and the growth she had achieved.

Jess's story was one of resilience and redemption, a testament to the power of truth and the importance of staying true to oneself amidst the chaos. As she looked toward the future, Jess was determined to continue her journey with clarity and integrity, ready to face whatever challenges lay ahead with renewed strength and purpose.

Chapter 12: Rebuilding

The world outside Jess Turner's apartment window was beginning to change with the arrival of autumn. The leaves had started their annual transformation, turning from green to shades of red and gold. It was a stark contrast to the turmoil Jess had faced over the past several months. The vibrant colors of the season seemed almost symbolic of the new chapter she was beginning—one of rebuilding and self-discovery.

After the dramatic revelations about Amanda and the additional conspirator, Jess had taken a significant step back from the public eye. The decision to temporarily withdraw from social media was both a relief and a challenge. She needed time away from the constant scrutiny and relentless demands of her online presence to regain a sense of self and rebuild her life.

The quiet of her apartment was both soothing and unsettling. Jess had spent so much of her life in the spotlight, her every move broadcast to millions, that the silence felt strange. She found solace in the stillness, using the time to reflect on her experiences and to begin the process of healing.

Jess's first priority was to reconnect with her family and mend the fractured relationships that had been strained by the scandal. The conversation with her parents had been a crucial first step, but the process of rebuilding trust was ongoing. She had arranged for family counseling sessions to address the underlying issues and to work through the emotional fallout.

The counseling sessions were intense, often bringing up difficult emotions and unresolved conflicts. Jess's parents were committed to the process, acknowledging their mistakes and expressing a genuine desire to repair their relationship with their daughter. Jess, in turn, was learning to navigate her feelings of betrayal and disappointment, striving to find forgiveness and understanding.

In addition to working on her family relationships, Jess sought to rebuild her connections with her friends. She reached out to those who had stood by her during the tumultuous period, expressing her gratitude and attempting to repair any damage that had been done. Reconnecting with her friends was a source of comfort and support, helping Jess feel less isolated as she worked through her challenges.

One of the most significant changes Jess made was in her approach to social media. Her break from the platform was not just a physical withdrawal but a mental and emotional shift. She used the time to reassess her values and priorities, focusing on what truly mattered to her beyond the superficial metrics of likes and followers.

Jess started to engage in activities that had once brought her joy but had been overshadowed by her online persona. She took up painting again, a hobby she had enjoyed as a child but had neglected in recent years. The process of creating art was therapeutic, providing a sense of accomplishment and a means of self-expression.

In addition to painting, Jess explored other creative outlets and personal interests. She began volunteering at a local community center, finding fulfillment in helping others and making a positive impact in her community. The work allowed her to connect with people on a more personal level, away from the scrutiny of her online persona.

As Jess continued to rebuild her life, she also made a conscious effort to address her own well-being. She sought professional help from a therapist to work through the emotional challenges she faced. Therapy provided a safe space for Jess to explore her feelings, develop coping strategies, and gain insights into her own behavior and motivations.

The process of rebuilding was not without its setbacks. Jess faced moments of self-doubt and frustration as she worked to reestablish her sense of identity and purpose. The journey was marked by periods of uncertainty and vulnerability, but Jess remained committed to her goal of personal growth and self-discovery.

One of the key aspects of Jess's rebuilding process was focusing on authenticity. She recognized the importance of being true to herself and embracing her genuine identity rather than the curated image she had presented online. This shift in perspective was both liberating and challenging, as Jess grappled with letting go of the persona she had carefully constructed over the years.

To support her new focus on authenticity, Jess began to explore new ways of connecting with her audience. Instead of relying on the superficial metrics of likes and followers, she sought to engage with her audience in more meaningful ways. She shared her journey of personal growth and the lessons she had learned, using her platform to promote positive change and authenticity.

Jess's efforts to rebuild her reputation and reconnect with her audience were met with mixed reactions. Some followers appreciated her honesty and the shift towards a more authentic approach, while others remained skeptical or disappointed. Jess understood that rebuilding trust and credibility would take time and that not everyone would embrace the changes she was making.

Throughout the rebuilding process, Jess found strength in the support of her close friends and family. Their encouragement and understanding helped her navigate the challenges and stay focused on her goals. The process of rebuilding was as much about restoring her relationships as it was about regaining her sense of self.

As the weeks turned into months, Jess began to see the fruits of her efforts. Her relationships with her family and friends grew stronger, and she developed a renewed sense of purpose and clarity. The time away from social media allowed her to gain perspective on her own life and the impact of her online presence.

Jess's journey of rebuilding was a testament to her resilience and determination. She faced the challenges head-on, embracing the opportunity to grow and learn from her experiences. The process was ongoing, and Jess knew that she would continue to evolve and adapt as she moved forward.

In the quiet moments of reflection, Jess recognized the profound impact of her journey. The challenges she had faced and the lessons she had learned had shaped her into a more self-aware and authentic individual. She had navigated the complexities of social media, deception, and personal growth, emerging with a renewed sense of purpose and a commitment to living a more genuine life.

As Jess looked towards the future, she felt a sense of optimism and hope. The journey of rebuilding had not been easy, but it had provided her with valuable insights and a deeper understanding of herself. Jess was ready to embrace the next chapter of her life with confidence and clarity, knowing that she had the strength and resilience to face whatever challenges lay ahead.

As Jess Turner continued her journey of rebuilding, she faced the reality that the path to recovery was neither straightforward nor easy. The end of her public scandal had brought about a complex mix of personal triumphs and ongoing struggles. Each day presented a new challenge, but also an opportunity for growth and self-discovery.

The decision to step away from social media had been one of the most significant and challenging choices Jess had made. For years, her life had been intimately intertwined with her online presence. Her every moment was documented, analyzed, and scrutinized by millions of followers. Stepping away from this constant visibility required a profound shift in her daily routine and mindset.

Initially, the absence of social media felt disorienting. Jess was used to the immediate feedback and validation that came with each post and interaction. Without the constant buzz of notifications, she had to confront the quieter, often uncomfortable reality of her own thoughts and emotions. It was a period of introspection and adjustment, where Jess had to learn to find validation and contentment from within rather than from the digital world.

In the weeks following her break from social media, Jess immersed herself in activities that fostered personal growth and fulfillment. She dedicated more time to her hobbies, such as painting and volunteering. The creative expression found in painting allowed Jess to channel her emotions constructively, while volunteering provided a sense of purpose and connection to her community. These activities were not just distractions but integral parts of Jess's healing process.

As Jess continued to rebuild her life, she faced the challenge of reestablishing her public image. The public scrutiny and judgment that had accompanied her scandal still lingered, and repairing her reputation was a gradual process. Jess recognized the importance of approaching this task with honesty and integrity. She began by selectively re-engaging with her audience, sharing her experiences and the lessons she had learned without reverting to the façade she had previously maintained.

One of the key aspects of Jess's rebuilding effort was transparency. She decided to address the public directly about her decision to take a break from social media and her journey through the aftermath of the scandal. In a carefully crafted statement, Jess acknowledged the mistakes she had made, the challenges she had faced, and the steps she was taking to make amends. This approach allowed her to control the narrative and present herself as someone who had learned and grown from the experience.

The reaction to Jess's statement was mixed. Some followers expressed understanding and support, appreciating her candidness and vulnerability. Others remained skeptical, questioning the sincerity of her efforts or continuing to hold onto past grievances. Jess accepted that regaining trust and credibility would be a gradual process, and she focused on staying true to her values rather than seeking immediate approval.

In addition to her public efforts, Jess placed significant emphasis on her personal relationships. Rebuilding trust with her family and friends was a priority, and she dedicated time to nurturing these connections. The family counseling sessions proved to be a valuable tool in addressing the issues that had arisen during the scandal. Jess's family worked together to repair their relationships, each member confronting their own mistakes and finding ways to support one another.

Her friendships, particularly with those who had stood by her during the difficult times, were also central to her rebuilding process. Jess made an effort to reconnect with friends and show appreciation for their support. She organized gatherings and reached out individually to express her gratitude and reaffirm her commitment to these relationships. This effort helped to strengthen her support network and provided a source of stability during the challenging times.

As Jess continued to navigate the complexities of her new reality, she also focused on personal development. She attended workshops and seminars on topics such as mental health, resilience, and effective communication. These experiences not only contributed to her growth but also equipped her with tools to handle future challenges more effectively.

Despite her progress, Jess still faced moments of doubt and uncertainty. The journey of rebuilding was not linear, and there were times when she questioned whether her efforts were making a difference. In these moments, she drew strength from her support network and the insights gained from her personal development efforts. She reminded herself of the progress she had made and the lessons she had learned.

One of the most significant realizations Jess had during this period was the importance of setting boundaries. Her previous experience had taught her the consequences of overexposure and the impact of allowing her life to be dictated by external validation. Jess began to establish clear boundaries between her personal and public life, ensuring that she maintained a healthy balance and prioritized her well-being.

As the months went by, Jess began to see tangible results from her efforts. Her relationships with her family and friends became stronger, and she regained a sense of stability and purpose. Her public image gradually improved as well, with positive feedback from those who appreciated her authenticity and the steps she had taken to address her past mistakes.

The journey of rebuilding was ongoing, and Jess knew that there would always be challenges ahead. However, she felt more equipped to face these challenges with resilience and clarity. The experience had provided her with valuable lessons about trust, truth, and the importance of living authentically.

Jess's story served as a reminder of the complexities of life in the digital age and the impact of social media on personal identity. Her journey of rebuilding was not just about restoring her reputation but also about finding a deeper sense of self and purpose. It was a testament to her strength and determination, as well as a reflection of the evolving nature of her relationship with the online world.

As Jess looked towards the future, she felt a renewed sense of optimism and hope. She had navigated the storm of scandal and emerged with a clearer understanding of her own values and priorities. The lessons she had learned would continue to guide her as she moved forward, embracing a more authentic and meaningful life.

Don't miss out!

Visit the website below and you can sign up to receive emails whenever Michael Ferguson publishes a new book. There's no charge and no obligation.

https://books2read.com/r/B-A-CKNW-ZWWZE

BOOKS 2 READ

Connecting independent readers to independent writers.

Did you love *Likes & Lies*? Then you should read *Cold Comfort*[1] by Michael Ferguson!

Dr. Henry Talbot once stood at the pinnacle of his profession, celebrated for his keen understanding of the human psyche. But his life unraveled after a scandalous affair with a patient, Emily Harper, led to his disbarment and descent into addiction. Now, two years later, Henry is a broken man clinging to the remnants of his former glory, haunted by Emily's mysterious disappearance.

When an anonymous note arrives, hinting that Emily is still alive, Henry's obsession reignites. Desperate for

---

1. https://books2read.com/u/mdanky

2. https://books2read.com/u/mdanky

redemption, he plunges into a perilous investigation, only to uncover a chilling conspiracy that links Emily's vanishing to a web of corruption within the mental health industry. As he delves deeper, Henry encounters a cast of characters, from shady rehab clinic patients to deceitful former colleagues, each harboring their own secrets.

The truth, however, is more twisted than Henry could have imagined. Emily's disappearance was a carefully orchestrated ploy to frame her abusive husband, Simon Harper, and dismantle Henry's career. In his relentless pursuit of justice, Henry realizes that Emily's manipulative brilliance used him as a pawn in a grander scheme of vengeance.

As the final pieces of the puzzle fall into place, Henry faces a heartbreaking decision: expose the full extent of Emily's betrayal and clear his name or shield her from the world's judgment, understanding the personal cost of his quest. Cold Comfort is a gripping tale of obsession, betrayal, and the devastating price of uncovering the truth. It explores the dark corners of the human mind and the lengths one man will go to seek redemption, even when it means facing the most harrowing truths of all.